Magical Animals
at Bedtime

Magical Animals at Bedtime

Tales of Guidance and Inspiration for You to Read With Your Child—to Comfort and Enlighten

Lou Kuenzler
Sandra Rigby
Andrew Weale

WATKINS PUBLISHING
LONDON

Magical Animals at Bedtime

First published in the UK and USA in 2013 by
Watkins Publishing Limited
Sixth Floor
75 Wells Street
London W1T 3QH

A member of Osprey Group

Managing Editor: Tania Ahsan
Editor: Krissy Mallett
Managing Designer: Luana Gobbo
Commissioned Artwork: Julia Woolf

A CIP record for this book is available from the British Library

ISBN: 978-1-78028-513-9
10 9 8 7 6 5 4 3 2 1

Typeset in Filosofia
Colour reproduction by PDQ
Printed in China

A NOTE ON GENDER
In the sections of this book intended for parents, to avoid burdening the reader repeatedly with
phrases such as "he or she", "he" and "she" are used alternately, topic by topic, to refer to your
child or children.

Distributed in the USA and Canada by
Sterling Publishing Co., Inc.
387 Park Avenue South
New York, NY 10016-8810
For information about custom editions, special sales, premium and corporate purchases,
please contact Sterling Special Sales Department at
800-805-5489 or specialsales@sterlingpub.com.

Contents

About This Book

Children seem drawn to animals wherever they encounter them. They adore the family pet and they love to stroke farm animals or visit the zoo. They're just as fascinated by animals in the wild. Children instinctively seem to want to connect with animals, to make friends with them, to share their world.

This may simply reflect the interest of the young in all that is different and new; but perhaps the significance of the bond between child and animal goes deeper. It's possible that a child's mind is more receptive to developing a connection with another living creature. The special relationship between child and animal is something to be cherished – it's a harking back to the ancient mysterious bond between animals and humans.

Up until the late 19th century, people in the West depended on animals for transport, for labour and for their livelihoods and well-being. In traditional hunter-gatherer communities the interdependent relationship between animals and humans was even more marked. In communities that are still free to live in their traditional ways, the deep respect animals command is profound.

In these communities animals take on the role
of guardians and spirit guides to humans and are
seen as providing essential truths about the world.
In such cultures animals truly are magical.

This book aims to help connect your child with the
wisdom and beauty of the world of animals. You'll find,
amongst many others in this menagerie, cats and
caterpillars, bears and birds, a kangaroo and a tortoise.
You'll also find animals celebrated in myths and legends
such as the beautiful mermaid, the phoenix that rises from
flames to be reborn and the unicorn – symbol of all that is
most pure and noble. These stories tell us not just about the
strength, courage and resilience of animals; they also
illustrate ideas important in a child's world as well. For
example, your child will discover how to have faith in his
abilities, how to persevere when things are difficult, and
how to work together with family and friends.

These magical animals are funny, endearing, wise and
beautiful. They're sure to become very special friends
whose adventures both you and your child will love to read
and re-read at bedtime.

Animals and Humans

Folk traditions from every culture around the world reveal the great importance animals have long held for humans. Animals have been recognized for their strength, their courage, their quick wits, their loyalty and their determination – qualities to which humans also aspire.

Shamanism

In hunter-gatherer cultures, animals perceived as having the greatest strength or prowess have often taken on the greatest significance in folk tradition. This can be seen, for example, in the importance of the bear in northern European nomadic cultures, where the word for "bear" and "warrior" are often one and the same. In shamanic cultures, which see the physical world infused with the spirit world, the line between human and animal is deliberately blurred. The shaman or wise man seeks to enter into a trance-like state that can help him take on the spirit of a particular animal. In Central Asian shamanism, this journey into the animal world is assisted by the shaman cloaking himself in a coat decorated with bird feathers and animal motifs and a cap made from the skin of a bird.

In many shamanic societies, animals are important guides for both the tribe as a whole and for the individual. In Native American cultures, the vision quest was a ritual whereby adolescents would journey to a remote site and wait to receive their "vision" from nature. Generally, a spirit guide taking the form of an animal will come to the child in a vision or dream and watch over their future life – bringing wisdom and insight.

Myth and legend

In many cultures, myths tell the story of humans who actually take on the characteristics of a particular animal in order to share their powers. For example, the ancient Greeks developed the idea of the centaur – half-man, half-horse – that had the speed and strength of an animal but the head and torso of a man. Ancient Egyptian mythology features many animal-headed gods including Anubis, king of the underworld, who was half-man and half-jackal. Meanwhile, Scottish tradition tells of the selkie – seal-like creatures who take on human form and even marry mortal men, before they inevitably return to the sea.

Animals are recognized for their cultural importance throughout world mythologies. Agrarian cultures depend fundamentally on the cow for life itself; the cow provides nourishment and plays a vital role in farming and transport. Accordingly, Hindus venerate every cow as the embodiment of the sacred cow, Kamadhenu, and allow them to roam freely about the streets. In Hindu mythology the bull, Nandi, is seen as the mount of the great god Shiva. The surviving remains of the culture of ancient Crete suggest that the bull was also a central figure in Minoan religious and cultural practice. Archaeologists have found artefacts including a bull's head rhyton (or vessel), which it's believed was used in sacred rituals. In ancient Egypt, the goddess Hathor embodied motherhood and femininity and was depicted either as a cow or with a pair of cow's horns on her head.

Aesop's Fables

Perhaps the most famous animal stories are Aesop's Fables or the Aesopica. It's thought that the stories were first told by Aesop, a slave and story-teller believed to have lived in ancient Greece between 620 and 560 BC.

Interestingly, nearly a dozen of Aesop's fables are also found in the Buddhist Jataka Tales and the Hindu Panchatantra, and some people speculate the fables are of Indian origin. The stories centre on the unique qualities of animals to teach us morals about our own behaviour. So, for example, in the story of the "Bear and the Bees" we learn how a bear's anger at being stung by one bee leads him to swat furiously at it, leading him to be attacked by a whole swarm. The moral of the story is that it's better to accept one injury silently than to bring about many injuries by reacting angrily. In the story of the "Lion and the Mouse", we learn how the kindness of a lion in releasing a mouse from his paws is rewarded by the mouse helping the lion escape from a hunter's net. The animal kingdom teaches us that "one good turn deserves another".

In every culture the myths associated with animals tell us much about the cornerstones of our own human society — what really matters to us and why. Over the following pages we look at some of the key animals celebrated in mythology around the world and explore what these animals can teach us today.

The Horse

One of the most potent animals in myths and legends from many lands has been the horse.

The Greek myth of Pegasus, the winged horse, is just one example of stories focused on the power and speed of horses. Pegasus was sired by the god Poseidon and ascended to Olympus where he carried lightning bolts and thunder for Zeus. It was said that wherever Pegasus' hoof struck the earth, a spring rich with inspiration for poets would burst forth. Pegasus is therefore associated with poetry.

The Greek hero Bellerophon rode Pegasus during many of his heroic exploits and even attempted to ride him to Mount Olympus. However, Zeus was angered by Bellerophon's boldness and caused the hero to fall from his steed all the way back to earth. The myth seems to suggest that the strength and beauty of the horse is so great that even when a great hero manages to ride the steed, his mastery is perilous and uncertain.

Pegasus has long been associated with wisdom and inspiration, and for the great psychologist, Carl Jung, Pegasus was the symbol of man's quest for spirituality.

The legend of a white horse that carries a great
end-of-time warrior to save the world is found in Hindu,
Christian and Muslim traditions, and the concept of the
chariot of the sun being pulled by white horses is common
to Norse, Celtic and ancient Indian and Greek mythologies.
England is also famous for the giant images of white horses
carved into chalk hillsides at Uffington in Oxfordshire and
Westbury near Salisbury Plain, and these images suggest
that the horse was of enormous significance to ancient
surrounding communities.

The unicorn, a white horse with a horn in the centre of
its forehead, is a fascinating development of the mythology
surrounding horses. During the Middle Ages, the unicorn
came to represent all that was most pure and holy, with the
unicorn often depicted resting its head in the lap of a
maiden. In this book, the story "The Princess and the
Unicorn" shows how a spoilt princess learns gentleness
and respect from the unicorn, an echo of the story of
Pegasus in which the proud hero Bellerophon has to learn
humility. The lesson we learn from horses is one of strength
but also one of grace and sensitivity.

The Bear

The bear has been held in reverence by both Northern European and Native American societies for thousands of years. In fact, there is evidence that early societies practised a kind of worship of the bear with many Siberian and Scandinavian cultures considering the bear to be an ancestor spirit. In many countries, such as Iceland, Sweden, Norway and Denmark, the word for "bear" is also a common boy's name suggesting the idea of a connection between the spirit of bears and that of humans.

In other cultures there is evidence that the word for bear was subject to a kind of taboo. Indeed, bears were considered to be so powerful that descriptive terms were used to denote the animal instead, such as "angry one" and "fur man". Viking traditions describe warriors who sought to take on the power and spirit of a bear by donning a bearskin shirt called a "bear-sark", which had been treated with oils and herbs. These warriors would become "berserk" through the power of the animal's spirit and were so ferocious in battle, they were said to be capable of biting through their enemies' shields.

In many Native American traditions the bear is similarly accorded great respect. Many tribes believed that the "Great Spirit" (the creator God) would often take on the form of a bear in the material world. For virtually every tribe the bear was a symbol of wisdom and strength, as well as being a creature that brought magical powers of healing and medicine. There were also many taboos about hunting bears during particular seasons so as to avoid killing a mother bear with her cubs. In some tribes, as in European traditions, it was forbidden to speak the name of the bear outside a ritual context.

Although bears are still common in parts of North America, their habitat has gradually been encroached upon and today bears and humans coexist uneasily. In this collection of stories, the tale of the "Little Black Bear and the Big Sleep" touches on the importance of understanding bears' habits and behaviours. Just like our ancestors, we need to learn once again to revere our fellow creatures so that we can live harmoniously with the natural world. The bear can teach us courage and power and the respect we need to show to nature.

The Tortoise

In many cultures around the world the tortoise is a symbol of steadfastness, wisdom and longevity – no doubt reflecting the great age tortoises can reach, as well as observing that they move slowly and steadily, meeting their needs through patience and a quiet strength. In a number of cultures including Hindu, Chinese and that of several Native North American tribes, tortoises or turtles were seen as bearing the weight of the world upon their backs – so great is their strength and reliability. According to Mohawk tradition, an earthquake is a sign of the World Turtle stretching to relieve the great weight she is bearing.

In Hinduism the World Turtle is called Kurma, with the earth seen as its lower shell, the atmosphere its body and the heavens its upper shell. In Chinese tradition the tortoise is one of the four fabulous animals that govern the points of the compass. The tortoise rules the north and is a symbol of endurance, strength and longevity, and was believed to have helped the god Pangu create the world. Tortoise shells were used for divination and it was believed that the upper part of the shell showed the signs for the constellations while the lower part related to the earth.

The tortoise was also an important animal for the Japanese, who associated it with immortal beings, good fortune, support and longevity, while in Vietnam the turtle is a central figure in myth and legend. One story recounts how the king of Vietnam offered the Chinese emperor a sacred turtle on whose shell was written all the events that occurred since time began. The Golden Turtle god, known as Kim Qui, is thought to have appeared at opportune moments throughout Vietnamese history. And at certain Taiwanese festivals, turtle-shaped cakes are made to ensure the year ahead is filled with harmony and prosperity.

In Aesop's Fables the story of the hare and the tortoise celebrates the patience and stamina of the tortoise in beating the hare in a race. The hare is arrogant and, confident of winning, takes a nap part way through the race, only to be beaten by the slow and steady tortoise.

The lesson of the tortoise is one of gentle resilience, a powerful message for both children and adults to absorb. In this collection, the story "The Tortoise's Birthday Trip" shows how quiet patience and endurance is rewarded by a wonderful adventure.

How Children Learn From Animals

Folk tales, myths and legends about animals have all been used traditionally in cultures around the world to provide insight, wisdom and guidance. The stories in this collection build on this tradition helping your child grow in maturity and knowledge through lessons from the natural world. However, in addition to reading the stories with your child, you may also like to consider some other ways to help your child gain new levels of understanding from animals.

City farms

Children growing up in the city generally have very limited exposure to the animals that underpin our way of life. City farms offer an opportunity for children to interact with animals such as sheep, goats, chickens and even cows. This allows children to discover our dependency on animals for food, clothing and so much that we take for granted. Children may be startled to learn that milk comes from cows rather than a plastic bottle or that the

sheep's back provides their woollen jumper, but these are essential facts to help build a child's sense of the interdependency between us and the natural world. City farms also allow children to appreciate first-hand the importance of animal welfare and to consider the conditions in which we raise the animals we rely on for food. As pressure for farming efficiency and the mass production of food grows, city farms can provide a timely reminder of the importance of respecting the welfare of the living creatures upon whom our own health and welfare depend.

Create your own farm

You may like to give some thought to the possibilities of animal husbandry in your own garden. Increasingly city-dwellers are exploring the options of bee-keeping, chicken runs and worm farms. These activities will help you and your child reconnect to nature and learn skills that our ancestors took for granted. Through a worm farm you can reduce your household waste and create a constant supply of compost for the garden, while chickens and bees will provide you with your own food supply.

Sponsoring an animal

Zoos and animal parks offer the chance to sponsor
endangered species and this provides an ideal opportunity
for young children to learn about the importance of nature
conservation and the protection of habitats. By sponsoring
an animal, a child can gain an understanding of the unique
beauty of a particular animal and learn about the threats to
the animal's environment. A sense of the interconnected
relationship between living things and the need to protect
what is rare and endangered will be an important lesson.

Animals in the wild

Take the opportunity to observe animals in nature with your
child. Buy a pair of binoculars to spot birds and other small
creatures without disturbing them and share regular
country walks with your child. Even in the city, parks and
gardens offer wonderful opportunities for wildlife spotting.
If you choose early mornings or evenings for your
explorations, you can be rewarded with special insights
into the secret life of the animals who share our world.

You can also show your child the amazing dexterity of birds in flight or the complex engineering skills of insects. You'll be demonstrating all that is precious and worthy of preservation in the natural world.

Animals at home

Looking after animal friends at home will help your child to understand the duty of care we have to domesticated creatures. Feeding, mucking out and grooming animals are the responsibilities that go hand-in-paw with the more fun aspects of playing and stroking our furry friends. If you live in an apartment and are unable to provide a home to a cat or a dog, you and your child can still enjoy the companionship of animals through offering to walk a dog for an infirm neighbour or house-sitting for a cat owner on holiday. If you decide to provide a home for fish, please do remember that they need lots of space and an outdoor pool covered with mesh wire to protect them – this is far kinder than a cramped fish bowl. Always ensure your child empathizes with the animals that share your home.

How to Use This Book

To help your child get the most from the stories in this book, it's important to ensure that she is calm and relaxed when you begin reading. Each story aims to provide a positive message and calming insights, helping your child pass gently into a refreshing sleep. To ensure the stories work their magic, take a little time to help your child become grounded and centred in the here and now. As she lies in bed, encourage your child to take three or four deep breaths and to relax her shoulders, neck and anywhere she may feel tension. You may like to massage her shoulders or temples gently to aid this process.

It's equally important for you to be as relaxed and calm as possible before you begin, so check that there is no lingering tension in your own body by taking some deep breaths. Try to shake off any dramas from earlier on in the day so that you are both solely concentrated on the stories.

The stories are designed to stimulate your child's imagination so be ready to respond to questions and explore flights of the imagination. Your child may find a story particularly resonant or appealing and want to apply it to her own life.

These journeys of self-exploration are important so encourage them as much as possible, and then when your child is ready, gently return her to the story you're reading.

Each story includes three insights that endeavour to take the meaning of the tales further and help your child relate the story to her own experience in a positive and meaningful way. Encourage your child to explore the insights as she wishes and see what you both learn about your child's world as a result. The aim is always to find ways in which to help resolve any challenges and worries from the day and bring about restful sleep.

At the back of the book you'll find visualizations and meditations to take your journeys further – each exercise aims to help you and your child draw closer to the natural world. You'll also find an index of values, which pinpoints the key themes and ideas that underpin each story.

Finally, remember that the stories in this book are for you and your child to enjoy and share together. Take the time to read slowly and remember to pause and watch how your child responds. The magic of story-telling will unfold gently for you both.

The Princess and the Unicorn

Relax, close your eyes and imagine you're walking in a beautiful forest. As you make your way through the ferns that grow underfoot, you're surrounded by tall trees and everything is dark and very quiet and still. Suddenly you see a magnificent pure white horse standing in a shaft of sunlight directly ahead. But this is no ordinary horse! This is the story of a princess who had everything she could possibly want and yet always wanted more … until she met a magical unicorn. Let's listen to her story.

Princess Poppy lived in a fine castle that was perched on a rocky crag at the edge of a deep, dark forest. Everyone said that Poppy was the prettiest princess who had ever lived. She had curly golden hair and eyes as blue as cornflowers and, if she could be bothered to smile, her teeth were like pearls. The problem was that Princess Poppy sulked and complained more often than she smiled. Nothing was ever good enough for her.

"The sun is too bright this morning," Princess Poppy moaned as she watched the maid draw back the curtains.

"Why have I nothing new to wear?" she raged at the lady-in-waiting who came to dress her.

"What? Only fifteen different kinds of pastries for breakfast?" she snorted at the butler at breakfast.

Everyone at court was fed up with Princess Poppy. Even though they all worked very hard to make her happy, she never said "please" or "thank you". If she was really cross she would scream and go red and kick her feet on the ground until she got her way.

Although she complained all the time there was one thing Princess Poppy did like and that was riding her pony, Strawberry. Every morning she would go down to the stables and John, the stable boy, would have Strawberry saddled up and ready. But one morning when Poppy went down to the stable, Strawberry was still in his pen.

"What's this?" shouted Princess Poppy. "Why isn't Strawberry ready for me?"

John came forward and bowed.

"I'm very sorry, my lady, but Strawberry's hurt his fetlock. That's his ankle, you know. He needs to rest and get better."

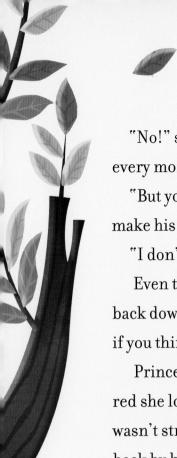

"No!" screamed Princess Poppy. "That's not fair! I ride every morning and I'm not going to stop now!"

"But your ladyship," said John, "riding Strawberry will make his injury worse. He might even go lame."

"I don't care," cried Poppy. "I'll do what I like."

Even though Poppy was shaking with anger John didn't back down. "I won't saddle him," he said. "It's wrong and if you think about it, miss, you'll see that I'm right."

Princess Poppy couldn't believe her ears. She went so red she looked like she might explode. But she knew she wasn't strong enough to lift the saddle onto Strawberry's back by herself and she couldn't ride him bareback.

"I'll show you! I'll get you into so much trouble," Poppy yelled. She turned and ran straight into the dark forest.

Princess Poppy ran and ran until she couldn't run any further. At last she flung herself down in the middle of some ferns. She kicked her feet and she beat her fists.

After a while Poppy stopped. No one was there to hear her. She looked around. She had come much deeper into the forest than she'd ever come with Strawberry. She realized, all at once, that she had no idea where she was. She had always relied on Strawberry to find the way home. Without him she was completely lost.

And that's when Princess Poppy became scared.

"How do I get home?" she wondered. "Who will help me?"

Poppy thought of the horrible things she'd said to John the stable boy. Would he look for her? And that made her think of the awful things she'd said to the lady-in-waiting and the maid and, well, practically everyone in the castle.

"Maybe no-one will want to find me," Princess Poppy suddenly thought. "All I do is shout at them all day long."

Finally Princess Poppy thought of how she'd been ready to ride poor Strawberry, even though he was injured, and she started to cry. "I've been so selfish. No one will come for me." Even though there was no-one there to hear her, she whispered, "I'm sorry, John. I'm sorry, Strawberry."

Suddenly Princess Poppy heard a whinny. She looked up and saw, standing in the sunlight, a beautiful white horse with a single horn of silver in the middle of its forehead.

"A unicorn!" gasped Poppy. She'd read about these creatures in storybooks but she had never thought they were real. Perhaps the unicorn might help her.

"If you please," began Poppy, as politely as she knew how. "I'm lost. Can you show me the way to my castle?"

The unicorn bent its head toward her. And then it slowly turned and trotted down a forest path.

Princess Poppy had to run to keep up. But she kept her eyes fixed on the beautiful pure white unicorn tail dancing before her. Soon the forest began to look more familiar. Poppy recognized an old oak tree and her castle beyond.

"Oh, thank you!" cried Poppy. But when she turned toward the unicorn, it had disappeared.

Princess Poppy ran as fast as she could to the stable.

"I'm sorry for being so rude," she said to John. "And I'm sorry, Strawberry, for being so thoughtless."

At first no-one at court could believe it was really Princess Poppy – she was so changed. But they grew to love their new, kind Princess and everyone agreed that she was no longer just the prettiest princess who had ever lived, she was the nicest too.

Inspiring Insights

- Sometimes we forget to notice all the good things in our lives. Take the time to value what you already have instead of always wanting more.
- Being rude to people makes them unhappy. Think about how you'd like to be treated and treat other people the same way.
- It's important to stand up for what you know is right, like John – especially when it involves protecting another person or an animal.

The Brave
Little Firefly

Relax, close your eyes and imagine a beautiful, tall tree with the most magnificent fiery red leaves. It stands at the edge of a forest by a tinkling stream. If you look very closely at the branches of the tree, you'll notice hundreds of tiny lights darting among the leaves. These are fireflies! This is a story about a very brave little firefly called Flash. Let's listen to his story.

Flash woke up and gave his wings a good stretch. He was excited because it was his first day at Firefly School.

"Have a good day," said Flash's mother as she gave him a little peck on the cheek.

"I will," said Flash, and he whizzed off from the patch of tall grass where they lived.

He flew up toward the highest branches of the red tree until he spotted his best friends, Sparkle and Lightning.

"I can't wait to start school!" cried Flash.

"Neither can I," agreed Sparkle.

"Well, let's stop dawdling and get in there!" said Lightning. "I'll race you!"

Lightning easily beat them to the leafy school gates. Their first lesson was Safety in the Sky. Flash learned how to turn right and left quickly without going into a spin, and how to avoid obstacles like branches and spiders' webs.

"This is such fun!" laughed Flash.

"Look where you're going!" cried Lightning. "You nearly flew into Sparkle!"

"Sorry, Sparkle," said Flash. "Maybe I need a few more of these flying lessons."

Their next lesson was Dangerous Creatures.

"I didn't know bats eat us for lunch," said Flash.

"And breakfast and dinner, too!" added Lightning.

"Ugh! They give me the creeps!" said Sparkle.

Then it was time for the lesson that everyone had been looking forward to: Finding Your Fire with Miss Fullbright.

"None of you have a fire in your tail yet," explained Miss Fullbright, "but you will find it."

"How did you find your fire, Miss Fullbright?" asked Flash.

"Well, one of my friends flew into a tree on our way home from school," began Miss Fullbright.

"He should have paid attention in class," joked Flash.

"Yes, he should," said Miss Fullbright with a smile. "But I was able to help him, and it was while I was helping him that the fire in my tail suddenly appeared."

"If I help someone," said Flash, "will I find my fire?"

"Maybe," replied Miss Fullbright, "but all of us are different. You'll find your fire in your own way."

"But how?" asked Flash.

"Well, you might find your fire by being very fast or very strong," explained Miss Fullbright. "It depends on what you're good at."

"I don't know what I'm good at," said Flash.

"Let's find out," said Miss Fullbright to the whole class.

They spent the rest of the morning doing exercises.

"I wonder who can fly the fastest!" cried Miss Fullbright.

Before the words were even out of her mouth, Lightning had zoomed off like a rocket. As he flew, a little orange glow appeared in his tail. Faster and faster and faster he went until the glow became a burning, golden fire.

"You found your fire, Lightning!" cried Miss Fullbright.

By the end of the lesson, everyone had beautiful golden fires glowing in their tails. Everyone except Flash.

"Don't worry, Flash," said Miss Fullbright reassuringly. "You'll find your fire, I promise."

Flash flew sadly from the leafy gates of the school.

"Everyone's going to laugh at me because I'm the only one without a fiery tail," moaned Flash.

"We're not laughing," said Lightning.

"You'll find it soon," added Sparkle. "I know you will."

Suddenly there was a rustle in the leaves ahead of them, and a huge bat burst out of the branches.

"Fireflies!" it cried, smacking its lips. "My favourite!"

Lightning and Flash whizzed away from the bat, but Sparkle wasn't quite fast enough.

"Mmm … you'll make a tasty snack," snapped the bat as it sped toward Sparkle.

Without even thinking, Flash swooped back toward Sparkle and shouted, "Hey, why don't you pick on someone your own size?"

"Good idea!" shouted the bat as it swooped away from Sparkle and started chasing Flash. "You're certainly much bigger and juicier!"

Flash zoomed around the red tree. The bat was close behind, and Flash could feel the air whooshing as the bat flapped its big wings. Just as the bat was about to catch him, Flash did one of the quick left turns he had learned in the Safety in the Sky lesson.

The bat was so surprised by Flash's sudden move that it crashed straight into the red tree.

"Ouch!" cried the bat, as it clattered through the branches down to the ground.

"Have a nice dinner," giggled Flash.

"Thank you!" cried Sparkle as Flash rejoined them. "You saved me from the bat."

"Wow!" exclaimed Lightning. "Look at your tail!"

Flash peered over his wing at his tail. It was burning with the most beautiful golden fire.

"I've found my fire!" whooped Flash.

"Yes!" said Sparkle. "And you found it by being brave!"

And at that moment, Flash was the proudest, happiest, and fieriest little firefly in the whole world.

Inspiring Insights

- You can learn a lot from your teachers. Flash listened carefully in class and used what he had learned to escape the bat.
- When our friends are feeling down, they need our support. Always encourage your friends, just as Lightning and Sparkle did with Flash.
- Sometimes our friends can do things more quickly than we can. If this happens, try not to get discouraged and lose hope.

Cedric the Centipede

Relax, close your eyes and imagine you're in a beautiful garden. At the bottom of the garden there's an old oak tree. If you bend down and look very carefully at the ground around the tree, you can see a tiny city called Bugsville. It's inhabited not by people like us, but by insects and other crawly creatures. Let's listen to their story.

Everyone in Bugsville was buzzing with excitement. The city's annual dance competition was only a day away, and all the creatures were busy practising their different dance routines.

The ladybirds were line-dancing and making beautiful patterns in the air. The grasshoppers were grooving and hopping all over the place. But one little centipede called Cedric, who had a very long body and more legs than he could count, didn't seem very happy. Cedric's legs never seemed to do what he wanted them to do, and every time he tried to dance he fell over with a deafening THUMP!

"Hey, everyone! Look at Cedric!" laughed the ladybirds. "He's invented a new dance called the Falling Over Foxtrot!"

Cedric went bright red with embarrassment.

"You'd better give up now," grinned the grasshoppers. "You haven't got a chance of winning the competition."

Cedric went even redder and crept away. He wanted to crawl under a stone and never come out again.

"They're right," said Cedric sadly. "I just can't dance!"

"Can't?" said a little voice. "Who said 'can't'?"

"I did," said Cedric. "And who are you?"

"I'm Sonia Silkworm." A worm with white, silky skin poked her head out from underneath a half-eaten leaf.

"Everybody can dance," said Sonia. "You just have to find the dance that's right for you!"

"All I can do is find the dances that are wrong for me," said Cedric sadly.

"I'm the greatest dance teacher in Bugsville," declared Sonia. "If anyone can find your dance, I can."

And they got down to work. The first dance Sonia tried to teach Cedric was the Tango, but his legs got into a complete and utter tangle. Next they tried the Twist – in this dance Cedric's legs got all jumbled up and it took all afternoon to untwist them. Finally, they tried waltzing together, but Cedric's legs flailed about so wildly that he nearly whacked Sonia on the head. By the end of the day, Cedric was covered in bumps and bruises.

"It's no good!" cried Cedric angrily. "I'll never be able to dance!" And he stamped his front feet in frustration. TAP!

"What did you just do?" asked Sonia.

"This!" shouted Cedric, and he stamped his feet once more. TAP!

"Do that again," said Sonia.

"With pleasure!" snapped Cedric, and he stamped his front feet a third time. TAP!

Sonia looked at Cedric with a big, silky smile and said, "Cedric, my dear, I think we've found your dance!"

It was the day of the dancing competition. The tiny patch of grass in front of the oak tree was full of little creatures waiting to see the dances. They were all fluttering with anticipation. All except Cedric — he was so nervous that his knees were knocking together.

"I ca-ca-can't do this!" he stuttered. "I can't possibly go out there and dance in front of everybody."

"Can't? Can't? Of course you can!" urged Sonia. "Just go out there and have fun!"

The band started to play. First on were the ladybirds. Cedric watched as they whizzed and swooped in wonderful circles in the air. Next, it was the turn of the bees, who showed off their ballroom dancing. And soon it was time for the final act.

"I now have a very special surprise," announced Simon Spider, the host of the show. "A big round of applause for the one, the only ... CEDRIC!"

Cedric could hardly move even one of his legs as he crept out onto the stage. Hundreds of faces were looking at him. Suddenly, one of the ladybirds shouted, "What are you going to do, Cedric? The-Falling-Flat-On-My-Face dance?"

Everyone in the audience started to howl with laughter. Cedric wanted to crawl off the stage, he was so embarrassed. But then the music started playing and something amazing happened. Cedric slowly lifted one of his front feet and tapped it on the ground. TAP! He tapped another one of his feet. TAP! He tapped two feet together. TAPPITY-TAP! He tapped 50 feet. And then he was tapping all of his 100 feet in time with the music. TAPPITY-TAP! TAP, TAP, TAP! Cedric had truly discovered his dance: it was tap dancing!

Soon all the other creatures were tapping their feet, too.

"This is such fun!" cried Cedric.

When the music was over he didn't want to stop.
He wanted to continue dancing. So he did! And everyone
carried on dancing with him.

"Well, the winner of this year's competition," announced
Simon Spider, "has to be … CEDRIC!"

Everyone started clapping and cheering.

"I just can't believe it," cried Cedric. "I've won first
prize!" And a huge smile stretched from one side of his face
to the other.

Everyone *can* dance. You just have to find your own
special kind of dance, like Cedric did. And if you ever want
a dancing lesson and you happen to be in Bugsville, then
pop into Cedric and Sonia's Dance Academy – maybe you,
too, will find your own dance there.

Inspiring Insights

- There may be something other people can do that you can't and vice-versa. Don't make fun of others just because they can't do something you can.
- If you work hard and don't give up, you can make your dreams come true.
- Sometimes our friends can see our talents better than we can. Listen to your friends when they tell you that you're good at something and be sure to tell them when you notice that they're good at something, too.

Jojo's Journey

Relax, close your eyes and imagine a beautiful cat with blue eyes. She has cream-coloured fur, dark pointy ears and a long, black tail. This is the story of Jojo, a spoiled Siamese puss. She belonged to a little girl called Jessica, who doted on her. Let's listen to her story.

Every morning Jessica poured milk into Jojo's special gold-edged cat saucer. Then Jessica went to the toy box and took out the ball of purple silk with an ostrich feather on the end. Jessica played feather games with Jojo all morning until the cat felt sleepy. Then Jessica carried Jojo to her basket in the sunniest spot by the window and stroked her tummy while her pet fell asleep.

"You're the best and most beautiful cat in the whole wide world," Jessica would always say.

"It's true," Jojo thought. "I'm a very beautiful cat."

Jojo would snooze in her basket and refuse to get up until Jessica served her cat nibbles in a silver bowl for tea.

Even if a mouse had run across the floor, Jojo wouldn't have twitched a whisker or shifted a paw.

"I don't need to chase mice," she thought. "I'm not a common moggy who has to hunt for my food. Jessica always brings me the very best of anything I want."

But one morning, everything changed.

"Get up!" said Jessica – rather rudely, it seemed to Jojo. "We've got a very busy day ahead."

Jojo purred and rubbed herself against Jessica's ankles like she always did when she wanted her morning milk.

"The refrigerator is empty," said Jessica. "You'll have to have water instead."

She filled an old chipped bowl from the tap. Where was Jojo's special saucer?

And what were those men doing? They were carrying the toy box outside to a van, and Jessica was letting them take it.

"This is such an adventure," Jessica cried. She was clapping her hands and talking excitedly.

The whole house was full of boxes and men in big boots. Everyone was busy. No one was paying any attention to Jojo. Not even Jessica. She was taking the pretty curtains down from the sunny window above the place where Jojo's basket was supposed to be.

"I've had enough of this," huffed Jojo.

She stuck her tail high in the air and marched straight out of the door.

"If Jessica's not going to play with me, I shall go outside and sit under next door's garden shed," she decided. "It may be dusty and dirty down there but it will teach Jessica a lesson when she notices I've gone."

All morning Jojo sat under the shed and sulked.

"A pedigree puss like me shouldn't be treated this way. I'm the best and most beautiful cat in the whole world," she fumed. "How dare Jessica ignore me? How dare she have something more important to do than to look after me?"

All morning Jojo waited for Jessica to call for her … but she never did. All Jojo could hear was the clatter of pans and the thump of boxes being piled into the van. She could make out Jessica's excited voice.

"They're all playing some sort of very silly game over there," thought Jojo. "And I don't like it! It has absolutely nothing to do with me."

Jojo curled her tail under her chin. She settled down among the dust and spiders' webs and went to sleep.

"Jojo! … JOJO! Where are you?" Jessica called in a desperate voice.

But Jojo didn't hear her. She was having a very important dream. Jojo was dreaming that she was queen of all cats, sitting high on a purple velvet throne.

"JOJO!" yelled Jessica.

Jojo twitched in her sleep.

Suddenly her eyes were wide open. Her heart was pounding uncontrollably. She flicked her ears, listening for the sound of the men and the thud of boxes. But there was nothing. Somewhere in the distance a van rattled away down the street.

Jojo scrambled out from under the shed. She leapt onto the garden fence. But Jessica's house was empty. There were no pretty curtains in the window, no van in the driveway ... and no sign of Jessica anywhere.

Jojo sniffed the air. For the first time in her life, she was thinking like a wild cat — with all the ancient art of a hunter.

"I'll have to find Jessica," she decided. "I was silly to sulk. Now she's left me behind."

Although the van had disappeared from sight, Jojo felt certain she knew which way to go. It seemed as if an invisible thread was leading her — and the purple ball of silk they always played with was magically tugging Jojo toward Jessica.

46

For three days and three nights, Jojo trudged along beside noisy roads. Her cream-coloured fur turned grey with dust. She drank muddy water from puddles. Once, she almost caught a mouse but it got away. She became hungrier and hungrier.

At last, Jojo came to a red house on the edge of a strange town. A pair of pretty curtains were hanging in the window.

"Jessica!" she purred and she flopped down, exhausted, on the doormat.

"Jojo!" cried Jessica flinging open the door. "I thought I'd never see you again."

She scooped the tired cat into her arms.

"You may be dusty," sobbed Jessica, "but you're the best, most beautiful ... most magical cat in the whole world."

Inspiring Insights

- We don't have to be the centre of attention all the time. By sulking and acting spoiled, Jojo got herself into very serious trouble.
- It can be upsetting when we don't understand what's happening. Instead of jumping to conclusions or getting angry, find out what's really going on.
- Jojo was upset when her routine changed but Jessica saw the excitement of moving house. A routine is lovely but a change can also be fun.

The Lonely Dragon

Relax, close your eyes and imagine you're deep inside a dragon's cave. All around you are glittering piles of gold coins, sparkling jewels and shiny, gold and silver goblets. This is the story of a dragon called Dimitri. He had huge green wings and a long tail like a serpent that was covered in spots. He could breathe fire and he had all the riches anyone could wish for. But Dimitri couldn't find the one thing he really wanted. Let's listen to his story.

Dimitri lived on a rocky island with 1,000 sheep, 1,000 goats and nearly 400 people who were all very scared of him. "What a great, long, scaly tail he has!" they would say. "What long, terrible claws! And when he breathes fire, why, he can burn an entire village to the ground!"

If Dimitri ever appeared outside his cave, the islanders would all run inside their houses, bolting the doors and windows. And every month they'd gather together a tribute for him — all the precious jewelry and gold they could find.

"Dragons love gold," they said. "Our tribute is the only thing stopping him from attacking us."

At first Dimitri enjoyed making everyone feel scared. "I must be very important," he thought to himself. "Everyone has to do exactly what I want."

Sometimes Dimitri played tricks on the islanders just to make them extra watchful. He would roar loudly, fly right over their houses, or breathe a mighty blast of fire that burnt all the shrubs in its path to a cinder. "What a terrible dragon," he heard the islanders say.

One day, Dimitri began to wonder if it might be better if people weren't so scared of him. He certainly liked the treasure that was brought to him every month. He liked how it sparkled and he loved the clinking sound it made as he swished his tail around it. But after a while that got boring.

One day Dimitri decided he would try to have a talk with some of the villagers. He flew down to the main village called Efeti and landed in the market square.

"Hello!" he shouted. "Is anyone there?"

But all the villagers stayed inside their houses quaking with fear. Dimitri gave up and flew back to his cave.

The next day Dimitri decided to fly out to sea. He had spied a fishing boat on the horizon and he'd had an idea.

"I'll help the villagers to fish," he thought. "I'll sweep up all the fish with my tail and guide them toward the fishing nets. Then the islanders will want to talk to me."

But when Dimitri flew toward the fishing boat, half the fishermen fell overboard in fright. Once everyone was back on board they started to row towards the island as fast as they could. "The islanders won't have any fish to eat today," thought Dimitri sadly, "and they'll all blame me."

For the first time, Dimitri felt how lonely he was. He would have given anything to have someone to talk to. "I don't want everyone to be scared of me," he thought. "And I don't want to be the most important person on the island. I just want to have a friend."

The next day a small boy called Spiros came to deliver Dimitri's gold. Spiros had been given the job because he was always being naughty. He'd play practical jokes and he was always telling everyone how strong and brave he was. "I'm not scared of a silly old dragon," Spiros would say.

Everyone got so fed up with Spiros's tricks and boasting that they all agreed he should be the person to deliver the dragon's gold. "It doesn't worry me," said Spiros, but he was shaking inside his boots as he reached the dragon's cave.

However, Spiros noticed something strange. Instead of fire, he saw clouds of steam rising out of the cave.

He drew a little closer to the cave mouth and peered in. At first Spiros couldn't see anything at all. Then, as his eyes adjusted to the light, he made out the most enormous mountain of treasure he had ever seen. Beside it, his head resting on his wing, was Dimitri. Spiros saw that the steam was coming from Dimitri's nose. The dragon was crying! His tears were trickling down his cheeks and turning his fire breath to steam.

At that moment Dimitri looked up to see the small boy staring at him. Someone had ventured into his cave! Someone had come to see him! He was so grateful he rushed forward eagerly and Spiros drew back in fright.

"Oh please don't go," pleaded Dimitri. "I don't want to hurt you. I'd just like to be your friend."

Spiros stopped in his tracks. "My friend?" he said. "No one wants to be my friend. No one likes me because I play tricks on them all the time."

"No one wants to be my friend, either." said Dimitri. "No one likes me because they're scared of me."

The boy and the dragon looked at each other. After a moment they both smiled.

From that day on Spiros and Dimitri became the best
of friends. Dimitri would take Spiros for rides on his back
so Spiros could see the whole island. Spiros and Dimitri saw
how hard the people worked in the fields and fished in the
sea, and were very sorry for all the trouble they'd caused.

Soon the little boy and the dragon were helping the
islanders all the time. With Spiros's guidance, Dimitri
helped them to fish and carry bundles of firewood.
Spiros and his dragon were so kind and so much fun
to be with that Spiros soon became the most popular boy
on the island. And everyone was so pleased with Dimitri's
help that they came to love and trust him.

"I don't want any treasure," said Dimitri, "I've got
friends and that is the most precious gift anyone can have."

Inspiring Insights

- Everyone gets lonely – even someone who seems to have everything they
  need. Always be ready to be someone's friend.
- It's easy to misunderstand people when you don't know them. Make the
  effort to reach out to others.
- Helping people is always a good way to find friendship. Look for the
  opportunities to help that might come your way.

The Night Flight

Relax, close your eyes and imagine you've gone to stay in a unfamiliar house. This is a story about a little boy called Eli who was afraid of the dark. Unable to sleep, he tossed and turned in his bed until an adventure made him face his fear of things that go bump in the night. Let's listen to his story.

Eli couldn't sleep at Grandma's house.

The night was full of noises.

SCRATCH! Was that a monster sharpening its claws?

CREAK! Was that an ogre opening the garden gate?

THUD! What was that?

Eli wanted to get out of bed and open the curtains to let in the moonlight. But it seemed so far across the strange, dark room to the window.

"I'll count to three," whispered Eli to himself, "then make a dash for it … one … two …"

Eli didn't move. He closed his eyes very tightly and wished he was at home.

"I'll count to five instead," he told himself.

"One ... two ..."

Eli shivered. "This is hopeless."

"Oh do hurry up, young man!" said a mysterious voice at the window.

Before Eli could even open his mouth to scream, a fluffy white owl swooshed the curtains open, swooped into the room and perched on the end of the bed.

"The name's Owlbert," hooted the bird, standing in the moonlight. "I gather you're having trouble sleeping?"

"Er ... well ... yes," said Eli, gasping for words.

"Tut tut! Can't have that," said Owlbert, shaking his wings. "What seems to be the problem?"

"I don't know," Eli blushed. He didn't want to admit he was afraid of the dark. Surely an owl would think that was absolutely ridiculous. But the wise old bird seemed to know everything already.

"I used to be afraid of the daylight," Owlbert hooted. "Imagine that. Sunshine scared the feathers off me!"

"Daylight's not scary!" laughed Eli. "You can see what everything is in the daytime."

"Hmmm," said Owlbert. "Do you know how my mother cured me? She took me for a daytime flight — through the clouds and sunshine. After that I wasn't scared anymore."

"Perhaps if I could fly through the night, I wouldn't be afraid of the dark," joked Eli.

"Exactly!" Owlbert swivelled his head right round so that he was looking straight into Eli's eyes. "Why else do you think I've come?"

Eli pulled the duvet up. His mouth dropped open.

"I'm going to fly? Tonight?"

"If you would stop jabbering and get on with it," said Owlbert. "I never heard such a twit-twoo about anything!"

"But ... " Eli swung his legs out of bed. "Even if I were brave enough to fly in the dark ... which I'm NOT ... it wouldn't work. I'm too big. And heavy!" he laughed. "If I climb on your back, you'll never be able to take off and fly."

"Who said anything about climbing on my back?" Owlbert sounded quite indignant. "Especially when you've got perfectly good wings of your own."

"Wings?" said Eli, but even as he spoke he felt a tingle in his arms like pins and needles. Bright white owl feathers burst through his pyjama top — instead of arms he had a pair of mighty wings. Instead of fingers ... feathers!

"Not bad!" said Owlbert. "Come on! We've got till the clock strikes midnight, and then you'll be tucked up back here without a feather in sight."

Before Eli could argue, Owlbert nudged him over to the window sill and out into the night sky.

"WOW!" cried Eli, swooping over the moonlit garden.

SCRATCH! A branch scraped against the shed roof.

"Before, I thought that sound was a monster sharpening its claws!" laughed Eli. The night wasn't scary at all now he was out in it. And flying was brilliant.

Eli learned to tilt his wings left or right to steer. A few strong flaps and he rose higher and higher, and then he could stretch out and glide. Over the village they flew.

"You're not doing badly," hooted Owlbert as they swooped along the empty High Street.

"Race you round the steeple!" cried Eli as they reached the churchyard.

"Just once," said Owlbert, his big eyes checking the church clock. "It's nearly midnight. I need to get you home."

As they flew back to Grandma's garden, Eli saw how small and snug the cottage looked nestled among the apple trees. There was nothing to be scared of here.

CREAK! The old garden gate blew in the wind.

"Before, I thought that was an ogre," laughed Eli.

He shot in through the window and landed in a heap as the clock struck 12. In a flash, the feathers vanished.

"That was AMAZING!" grinned Eli. "I'll never be afraid of the dark again now that I know what it's like to be an owl."

"Very wise," said Owlbert. "Now I must be going."

" But," Eli said nervously. "I know what the SCRATCH! was. And the CREAK! But what was that THUD! I heard?

"Ah ..." Owlbert pretended to preen his feathers. "That might have been me. I misjudged my landing and toppled out of an apple tree when I arrived."

"So there's nothing to be scared of," laughed Eli, "... unless I stand under a tree and get hit by a falling owl!"

Inspiring Insights

- Unfamiliar places can seem a little scary because you don't know what to expect — but don't let that spoil the adventure of being away from home.
- Laughing or thinking of something funny can make you feel less nervous. Make up a silly story about something you're afraid of ... it might not seem so frightening then.
- People are scared of different things — just like Owlbert was afraid of daylight.

Gopal and the Mermaid

Relax, close your eyes and imagine that you're lying on a sandy beach in the shade of a palm tree. The sea is a glittering brilliant blue and gentle waves are lapping the shore. This is a story about a poor boy called Gopal, who lived in the south of India by the sea. Gopal had to fish all day to help feed his family and there was no time for school. Life was very difficult until one day Gopal met the most amazing creature. Let's listen to his story.

Gopal sighed deeply as he sat on a rock ledge above the sea, his fishing net dangling in the water. He'd been here for hours hoping for a catch but had had no luck. Gopal was worried. He had four younger brothers and sisters who would all be hungry tonight if he didn't catch anything. Gopal's mother would make chapati and cook some rice but that only went so far — everyone was longing for some delicious fish to fill their bellies. Gopal's father worked hard on a fishing boat all day and came back very tired.

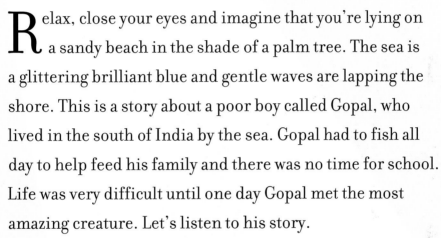

He had to share his catch with three other fishermen on the boat and there was never enough to go around. Gopal's father was always hungry when he got home but he and Gopal's mother always gave most of their food to the younger children.

Each morning his mother said, "Go to the beach, Gopal, and see if you can catch us some extra fish for dinner."

Gopal should have been in school, but he knew how hungry his little brothers and sisters were and so he would go to the beach with his net. But today he had caught nothing. It was late in the afternoon and it looked as if he was going to have to return empty-handed.

"Please, fish," whispered Gopal, "please swim into my net." But nothing happened at all.

Sadly, Gopal packed up his small net, hoisted his empty bucket over his arm and got to his feet to make his way back home along the seashore. Just then he heard a splash not far away and turned to see a greeny-blue fish tail disappear beneath the waves.

"Wow, that was a big fish," Gopal exclaimed. "But it was far too big for my net."

He kept gazing at the sea and then a moment later there was a very big splash.

Gopal couldn't believe his eyes. A girl with long, golden hair bobbed up from below the water and looked at him; with another splash she disappeared.

"Surely it can't be a mermaid," wondered Gopal out loud to himself. "Not really."

"Why not?" said a tinkly voice close to his ear. The girl with golden hair surfaced very close to the rocks, not more than a foot from where Gopal sat. She fixed her eyes on his and they were the deepest blue that Gopal had ever seen. They were the colour of the sea.

"Don't you believe in mermaids?" she asked.

"Well – I – well," spluttered Gopal.

"My name is Pearl. I watch you every day," said the mermaid. "I tell the little fish to keep away from your net."

"To keep away?" cried Gopal. "But how am I to feed my family if I can't catch any fish? There are so many of us, and the little ones are often hungry. And I'm often hungry, too." Big tears started to roll down Gopal's face.

"There now, don't cry," said Pearl. "I don't want you all to go hungry. But you humans can be greedy. We fish folk are very wary of you."

Gopal sat down and blinked away his tears while Pearl looked at him thoughtfully.

"I will help you," she told him at last. "But in return you must make three promises."

"Of course," said Gopal. "If I can, I will."

"First I want you to come on a journey under the sea with me. I want to show you my underwater realm."

"Underwater? I won't be able to breathe," said Gopal.

"You must trust that I will keep you safe and well," said Pearl. "Are you ready? Come, take my hand."

And before he knew it, Gopal was swimming deep in the sea, passing crabs and seahorses and sea urchins and so many fish – silvery fish and blue and yellow striped fish and red fish. They were so lovely, gliding silently by. The next minute Gopal and the mermaid had surfaced by the rock ledge and he clambered back ashore.

"Now," said Pearl, "I want you to promise to remember everything you have just seen; how beautiful it was, how rich and precious. The second promise I ask of you is that you never be greedy as a fisherman but only take as much as you need and no more. The sea world is fragile and the more you take, the more fragile it becomes."

Gopal thought about how beautiful the fish were in their home and how he would hate to see them disappear.

"Yes, I promise," he said.

"And the last thing I ask," said Pearl, "is that whenever you take a fish from the sea, you give thanks for the gift you've been given and honour it."

"I will," declared Gopal solemnly.

And from that day on, Gopal found that the fish swam into his net and he could take food home for his family. He didn't need to fish all day anymore – just for a short time in the morning. After that he went back to school to study. His mother and father were very proud of their kind and wise son, who worked hard and helped them all.

And every so often, usually late in the afternoon, Gopal would sit on the rock ledge and catch a glimpse of a golden-haired girl far out to sea, who would disappear into the glittering waves with a flick of a fish tail.

Inspiring Insights

◇◇◇◇◇◇◇◇◇◇◇◇◇◇◇◇◇◇◇◇

- The natural world is a special place. Always look after it.
- Although it can be tempting to take as much as you want, it's better to leave plenty for everyone to share.
- It's good to recognize when you've been given a gift – even if it might seem free. Give thanks for the good things that come to you each day.

Little Black Bear and the Big Sleep

Relax, close your eyes and imagine a huge forest deep in the heart of America. In this forest many different kinds of animals live together. There are small animals such as mice. There are bigger, fiercer creatures such as wolves. Now, imagine an animal that's even bigger than a wolf. It has thick black fur, large paws and a snout – it's a bear! This is a story about a little black bear called Growl who never felt sleepy. Let's listen to his story.

Growl lived with his mother in a cave on the side of a small mountain. He loved to play hide-and-seek with his friend Rumble in the trees and among the rocks.

When it was time for bed, he never wanted to go to sleep.

"Tell me one more story," he would beg his mother.

"I've told you two stories already, my little one," his mother would reply.

"Just one more. PLEASE!" Growl would plead.

Slowly the hot summer turned into autumn.

Growl helped his mother gather lots of branches and leaves for their cave.

"Why do we need so many leaves and branches, mother?" asked Growl.

"Because soon, my little one, we're going to have a very big sleep," replied Growl's mother, "and we need to make our bed as soft and comfortable as we can."

"A big sleep?" said Growl with a tiny twitch of his nose. He didn't like the sound of that. "How big?"

"We'll sleep all through the winter," replied his mother.

"All through the winter!" cried Growl. "But that's like forever and ever. Why do we have to sleep through the whole of the winter?"

"Because the winter is dark and cold and the forest isn't safe," warned his mother.

"So what if it's dark and cold," said Growl. "I don't want to go to sleep for the whole winter."

Soon there was ice in the air and a bitter wind scoured the forest. The days grew dark and the wolves howled hungrily in their lairs. The time had come for the bears to close their eyes and go to sleep for the winter.

"Please tell me one more story," pleaded Growl as he lay with his mother on their soft bed of leaves.

"I have told you six stories already," yawned his
mother sleepily. "Now snuggle up to me and try to
close your eyes ..."

"But I don't want to close my eyes," said Growl.

His mother let out a big snore.

"Don't go to sleep!" cried Growl, giving his mother
a little nudge with his nose. "I want to hear another story."

But his mother let out another big snore, much louder
than the first. The big sleep had begun but Growl was
still wide awake.

Growl got up and padded over to the mouth of the cave.
Little flakes were falling from the sky and whirling in the
wind. The ground was dazzling white.

"What's that?" wondered Growl.

He'd never seen snow before.

He swiped at one of the flakes with his paw. It felt cold
and tingly on his skin. Then he poked his head outside the
mouth of the cave and some more white flakes landed right
on the tip of his nose.

"This is fun," laughed Growl.

He took a step outside.

"Wow, look at that!" exclaimed Growl. "I can make
patterns with my feet."

He bounded out of the cave.

"I must go and find Rumble," he cried. "She'll love this!"

He skipped down the hill to the cave where Rumble lived, sending up sprays of white powder snow as he went.

"Rumble!" he shouted, when he got to her cave.

There was no answer.

"Rumble!" he cried again. "You've got to see this."

The only answer this time was a little snoring sound.

"Oh, no … you can't sleep now," cried Growl. "Wake up!"

A slightly louder snore came from inside the cave.

"Spoilsport," said Growl sulkily. "Well, I'll just have to have fun all by myself."

Growl kicked at the snow with his feet, but it wasn't going to be much fun playing without Rumble. The snow was ice cold and the wind was biting more sharply. Growl gave a little shiver. Suddenly, he heard a noise.

AwOOOoooo!

It was joined by another howl, sad and lonely … followed by another.

AwOOOoooo!

It was a pack of wolves. Growl shivered. Not with cold this time, but with fear. The forest wasn't safe with wolves around.

AwOOOoooo!

The howling was getting closer and Growl was all
by himself. Suddenly being awake and outside in the
cold, dark forest didn't seem like such a good idea after all.

AwOOOoooo!

Where could he go to be safe and warm? The answer
came into his head so quickly he could hardly move his feet
fast enough up the hill. He burst out of the cold into his cave.
He dived onto the bed of leaves with his mother and
snuggled up to her thick, warm fur.

The cold winter wind moaned outside but Growl felt
warmer and safer than he'd ever felt before. He snuggled up
even closer to his mother and closed his eyes. He let out a
little snore. And finally Growl fell asleep.

Inspiring Insights

- It's good to help around the house. Growl helped his mother collect leaves
  and branches for their cave – could you be as helpful?
- You should listen carefully to adults, especially when they're telling you
  something important. Growl learned the hard way that the forest wasn't safe.
- You may not feel sleepy, but your parents may be very tired. Don't be upset if
  they can't read another story — especially if they've just read this one to you!

The Acacia
Tree Friends

Relax, close your eyes and imagine it's the end of a long, hot day in Africa. The sun is setting and the trees cast shadows on the ground. This is the story of a little cheetah cub who only liked to play games that she could win. Let's listen to her story.

In the cool evening, Cheetah came bounding up to the old acacia tree where she always met her friends.

"Hello," she called to the baby monkey who was hanging upside down in the branches. "Where's Snake?"

"Boo!" said little Snake, popping out from a pile of leaves.

"Argh!" Monkey toppled backwards off his branch. "You gave me a fright!" he cried.

"I was hiding!" grinned Snake, flicking her tongue.

"Well, stop hiding and come and race!" said Cheetah. "I'm so fast. You know I'll win!"

"We race every day!" sighed Snake.

"Let's tell jokes instead," giggled Monkey.

"No," said Cheetah. "I want to race... ready, steady, go!"
Before the others could stop her, Cheetah charged off.

"First one to the water hole wins!" she yelled.

"That's not fair!" shouted Monkey, bounding after her.

"We weren't even ready," complained Snake.

No matter how fast Snake slithered or how quickly
Monkey ran, they could never catch up with Cheetah.

"I'm the fastest animal ever!" she boasted. They raced
all evening and Cheetah always won.

"Let's do something different tomorrow," suggested
Snake. "I don't want to race all the time."

"Racing is best!" declared Cheetah. "See you tomorrow!"

But the next day her friends were nowhere to be found.

"Monkey?" she called. "Snake?"

There was no answer. Cheetah looked everywhere and
was about to give up when Monkey giggled above her head.

"What are you doing?" Cheetah called.

"Playing hide-and-seek," chuckled Monkey high up in
the branches. "Now we have to find Snake."

Finally, they spotted Snake curled around the tree trunk.
Her speckled skin looked just like bark.

"Found you!" cried Cheetah. "That was fun.
But I still like racing best."

"That's because you always win," explained Snake. "Sometimes it's good to do things other people enjoy."

"I'm sorry," said Cheetah. "I'll play your game."

The three friends played hide-and-seek all evening. Snake was best but Cheetah was pretty good, too. Her spots made perfect camouflage in the long grass.

"And now for a joke," grinned Monkey. "Why should you never play cards in the jungle?"

"Why?" asked the others.

"There are too many cheetahs!" laughed Monkey.

Everyone groaned. But they listened to his jokes whenever they met at the acacia tree ... and they played hide-and-seek ... and had running races, too. After all, they were the very best of friends.

Inspiring Insights

- Having a special talent is great but it's good to find out what your friends enjoy and join in with them, too.
- If you're bossy, people may not want to play with you. Cheetah's friends were getting a bit fed up with her until she did what they wanted for a change.
- Your friends' hobbies can often be fun for you. Cheetah found she was good at hide-and-seek as well as running.

The Flight of the Condor

Relax, close your eyes and imagine you're climbing up the steepest mountainside you've ever seen. You're so high up that you can see wisps of clouds below you. You're following a path of ancient stone steps to reach a ruined city at the very top of the mountain. This is the story of a girl called Claire who also made that climb. But she needed the help of a giant bird called a condor to get home safely. Let's listen to her story.

Claire was very excited when her mother and stepfather told her about the holiday they were planning. They were going to walk the trail of an ancient people called the Inca to one of the most amazing archaeological sites in the world.

But Claire was not so pleased when she heard that her older stepsister, Lizzie, was going to be coming with them. Lizzie was 15 and Claire, who was only 11, felt that she was always being bossed around by her. What's more, Lizzie got all the attention because she was always so grumpy.

Claire's mother and stepfather were constantly trying to cheer Lizzie up and often seemed to forget Claire was there at all. Sure enough, as they set out for their four-day hike with a group of other walkers, Lizzie began complaining about how her boots were giving her blisters and how steep the climb was and how she wished that the trip was over.

"But we're so lucky to walk this trail," said her father. "This track was built by the ancient Incan civilization many hundreds of years ago and we're walking in their footsteps."

"The track leads to a ruined city standing in one of the most beautiful places on Earth," added Claire's mother.

"Boring!" moaned Lizzie.

The higher they climbed into the steep mountains, the slower Lizzie walked and the more she complained.

"No-one pays me any attention, even though I'm being really good," thought Claire. "I bet no-one would notice if I disappeared altogether."

The next day they were due to reach the ruined city called Machu Picchu. Claire felt very excited as she laced up her hiking boots. "I'm not going to wait for silly Lizzie dragging her feet," she thought to herself.

She said to her mother, "I want to walk at the front of the group today, Mum. Is that alright?"

"I'd rather you stayed with us," replied her mother. "That way we can all share the experience as a family."

But just at that moment Lizzie let out a piercing scream. "There's a spider in my boot," she yelled. Her mother turned to look and Claire called, "See you later, Mum," and raced ahead to the front of the tour group.

Claire liked being at the front. She kept pace with Bill, the tour guide, who told her the names of the mountains and pointed out rare flowers and animals. It wasn't long before Machu Picchu appeared before them.

"It looks like it's floating in the sky," thought Claire as she gazed at the city's stone walls and platforms. It seemed to hang like a balcony on the side of a mountain peak, the ground dropping away steeply in every other direction.

"If only I could climb a little higher I could get an even better view," Claire thought. "And if I went alone, I'd have it all to myself with no-one to spoil my enjoyment."

Just then, Claire spied narrow stone steps leading away from the tour group and up a slope. "This will take me to where I need to go," thought Claire, and she began climbing.

The path grew steeper and narrower, but Claire kept climbing until she reached the summit and could see the peaks of the Andes mountain range stretching below her.

"Wow!" gasped Claire.

All of a sudden she felt faint and unsteady on her feet. She became frightened of falling down the mountain slope. "It's so steep," Claire thought, "how will I get back down?"

And then Claire realized that no-one knew where she was. She'd set off without any warning, and neither her mother or stepfather, nor the tour guide, knew she had climbed the mountain path. She was so high up that no-one would hear her if she called out or see her if she waved.

"Why didn't I tell anyone where I was going?" wailed Claire. "I wish I'd stayed with Mum and Dad – and even Lizzie." And Claire began to cry.

At that point she became aware of a shadow overhead. She looked up and saw that it was a condor – an enormous bird that her mother had told her was sacred to the Incas. "They called it the god of the sky," her mother had said and Claire could understand why. The condor circled above her, riding the air currents with its vast black wings fully spread.

"Please help ... maybe you really are a sky god," whispered Claire. "I'm dizzy and afraid and I don't know what to do."

The condor continued to fly slowly round and round above her and eventually Claire grew calmer. "It will be alright," she told herself. "Everything will be okay."

And soon she saw the tour guide coming up the track.

"Claire!" Bill called. "Thank goodness we've found you. What are you doing here? Your family are frantic with worry."

"I'm sorry," said Claire. "I got excited and climbed this path I found, but it was so steep I couldn't get down again. But how did you know where to find me?"

"I didn't know where you were," said Bill. "But I spied the condor circling overhead and something made me follow it. It seems to have led me to you."

That evening Claire's family all sat close to her and didn't let her out of their sight. But Claire wanted to stay with them, too. Going off on an adventure by herself had been exciting for a while, but she'd rather share her adventures with other people next time.

Inspiring Insights

- Sometimes you have to share your parents' attention but that doesn't mean they love you any less. There's always plenty of love to go around.
- Going off by yourself can be dangerous, especially if you don't tell anyone where you're going. Often it's more fun to share experiences with others.
- When you're in strange places you may be tested in unusual ways. It's best to stay with someone who knows the area and who can help you.

The Extra-Slow Wombat

R elax, close your eyes and imagine you're in a snug burrow on the side of a wooded hillside. You can hear the wind in the trees and the sound of water tinkling in a stream. This is a story about an Australian animal called a wombat, who came last at everything. Wombats are a bit like badgers, only bigger and slower. This particular wombat, Ronald, wasn't the smartest animal that ever lived, but he was one of the nicest. And one day he had to do something really heroic. Let's listen to his story.

Ronald paused at the entrance to his burrow and sniffed the air. It was cold at dusk in his home up in the valley, but he liked how fresh and clear it felt. His furry coat kept him warm and his burrow was cosy and dry — just the right sort of place to come home to after an evening foraging for food. He ventured out a little further and made his way down toward Tumbledown Creek for a drink of water before he began his night's work.

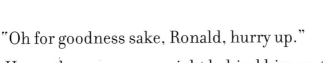

"Oh for goodness sake, Ronald, hurry up."

Henry the possum was right behind him on the trail to the stream and was getting impatient. Ronald knew he was very slow, but he couldn't help it. He only had short legs and although he tried to keep himself trim, wombats aren't naturally slim creatures. Possums can scamper along the ground and jump from tree branches. But Ronald just had to chug along at his own pace.

"I'm very sorry, Henry," said Ronald. "I don't mean to slow you down."

But Henry just tut-tutted and raced ahead as soon as there was space on the path to overtake.

Suddenly Henry stopped short so quickly that Ronald bumped right into him. There was quite a gathering of animals in a clearing ahead. Three or four small kangaroos called wallabies were there, ears twitching. And then there were five or six more possums, as well as a kind of porcupine called an echidna, whose name was Errol. Kevin the kookaburra, a large bird, sat in a tree overhead and the koala bear couple, Margaret and Claude, sat on the ground. All the animals were talking nervously.

"What's wrong?" asked Ronald as he drew near.

"Ronald, don't you ever pay attention?" said Kevin.

"We've been talking about this for days. That new road the humans have built right in front of the stream is really dangerous. Poor Errol was nearly hit by a car last night."

"That's right," said Errol. "I was following my favourite supper of ants across the road when I was blinded by lights. Next thing I knew, the car was nearly on top of me. I curled up into a ball and somehow it missed me."

"Claude and I don't dare cross the road," piped up Margaret. "The cars go so fast we just don't have a chance. But our favourite gum tree is on the other side of the road. It has the most tender leaves; the best for eating. What are we to do?" Margaret started to cry.

"Please don't cry," said Ronald, and he gave Margaret a comforting nuzzle with his snout. "We'll sort something out."

"And what would that be, numbskull?" sneered Kevin. "We all need to drink from the stream. I've tried keeping a lookout from high up in my tree in order to signal when it's safe to cross, but the cars go so fast that it's no use."

"Well, we mustn't give up hope," said Ronald.

"Oh, you make me so angry," yelled Rico, the wallaby. "What suggestion would a stupid, slow wombat like you have? Even for us fast animals it's not safe to cross that road ... it's just hopeless."

Ronald turned for home. He knew everyone was upset and worried and that's why they had spoken so unkindly, but there had to be a solution. He returned to his burrow and made himself comfortable. He knitted his brow, rested his head in his front paws and thought as hard as he could. And finally, after thinking for several hours, Ronald had the solution. He would do what wombats do well — he would dig! He would dig a deep tunnel under the road so that all the animals could use it to cross to the stream. It would take him a long time but he would do it in the end.

And that's just what Ronald did. Every night and every day he tunnelled with his front paws and brushed away the soil with his back paws. At first the other animals laughed at him. Kevin the kookaburra laughed the loudest.

"So you're going to make a tunnel big enough even for the wallabies? I doubt it!" squawked Kevin.

But gradually the other animals saw that Ronald was making progress.

"I'm going to help," said Errol the echidna. "I can dig, too. And many paws make light work."

"We'll help as well," offered Margaret and Claude. "We can carry some of the soil away, and then when Ronald and Errol are tired we can take over to give them a rest."

Soon the wallabies were joining in, using their strong back legs to push away the dirt. Before long the tunnel was ready and all the animals could reach the stream safely.

Rico the wallaby went to have a drink, but Margaret the koala stopped him.

"No," she said. "The first drink belongs to Ronald. Thanks to his hard work and clever thinking we can all drink safely. Three cheers for Ronald, the most brilliant wombat that ever lived!"

And all the animals, even Kevin the kookaburra, let out three great cheers.

"Gosh," blushed Ronald. "Thank you very much, it wasn't anything really."

But actually he was very pleased and proud.

Inspiring Insights

◇◇◇◇◇◇◇◇◇◇◇◇◇◇◇◇◇◇◇◇◇◇◇

- Have faith in yourself. It isn't necessary to believe everything other people may say about you.
- People sometimes say mean things when they're worried. Try to understand how others are feeling and why they're behaving in a certain way.
- Big problems can become small problems when you get help. Don't give up when you don't know what to do – like Ronald, you'll find a way in the end!

The Smallest
Pony

Relax, close your eyes, and imagine you're as light as a feather. This is a story about a small pony with a secret, magical gift. Let's listen to his story.

Emily and her brothers were staying on their uncle's farm. William and Philip were older than Emily, and Uncle Jim let them ride beautiful horses over the moors.

"Goodbye," Emily called as her brothers cantered away.

"See you, Squirt," teased Philip.

William waved and stuck out his tongue.

"I hate being the youngest," sighed Emily. "I never get to do anything fun."

"Don't look so glum!" said Uncle Jim. "I've got the perfect friend for you."

He pointed to a pony so small he couldn't even poke his nose over the stable door. He had big black and white spots as if someone had spilled a pot of paint over him. He was as shaggy as a bear.

"Oh dear," thought Emily. How William and Philip would laugh if they could see this scruffy little thing. They'd say he was a baby's pony.

"Meet Patch," smiled Uncle Jim. "He doesn't look like much, but he's a lovely ride."

"Really?" Emily frowned.

"Don't judge a book by its cover!" chuckled Uncle Jim.

"What does that mean?" asked Emily.

"It means you shouldn't make up your mind by looks alone," Uncle Jim explained. "Take the time to get to know things first. Why not go to the paddock? Ride Patch and see how you get on."

Emily rode Patch gently in a circle. His legs were short but there was a spring in his step.

"Good boy," she smiled. She urged him gently forward with a squeeze of her legs.

Patch began to trot.

"You're so much faster than I thought," she said.

Patch shook his head happily as if he understood what Emily was saying.

Suddenly, there was a great whooshing sound and two magnificent white wings spread out on either side of the saddle.

"Whoa!" cried Emily as the tiny pony rose up in the air. "You can fly!"

Emily clung on tightly to Patch's mane as the little pony flew over the paddock gate. They soared over the farmhouse and high above the moors.

"I feel like a bird!" cried Emily as they skimmed the top of the trees. The wind was blowing in her hair.

Far below, she saw William and Philip, galloping up the hill toward the farmhouse. They looked like tiny toys.

"What you need is wings!" called Emily. But the boys didn't even see her so high in the clouds.

Patch looped the loop and landed back at the farm.

Emily patted her incredible pony and said with a grin, "Thank you, Patch. That was the best ride ever!"

Inspiring Insights

◇◇◇◇◇◇◇◇◇◇◇◇◇◇◇◇◇◇

- Take time to get to know about something or someone before you decide what you really think – it's easy to get the wrong idea if you rush.
- Things that seem disappointing at first can often turn out to be good fun.
- Often we're influenced by other people's opinions but they don't always know best. Emily was worried about what her brothers might think about Patch but, in the end, their opinion didn't matter.

The Cuckoo and the Worm

Relax, be very still and imagine a beautiful little cuckoo. He wasn't a real cuckoo. He didn't eat worms and fly in the sky like other birds. He was a wooden cuckoo and he lived in a large wooden cuckoo clock, which stood in the main square of a small town. Let's listen to his story.

Every hour the cuckoo flew out of the clock and sang "Cuckoo!" He was so good at his job that no-one in the town bothered to wear a watch. They just listened out for his song.

The cuckoo considered himself very lucky indeed. He had a good job and he lived in the grandest clock in the town. But the cuckoo also had dreams. He had overheard the birds that twittered on the roof above his head. They spoke about wonderful places called forests, which were full of trees. There, birds could live and fly and be free. How he would love to leave the clock and go there!

One day, just before three o'clock, he heard a noise. MUNCH! MUNCH!

"I wonder what that is?" said the cuckoo.

He looked all around him but he couldn't see where the noise was coming from. A few minutes later he heard the sound again.

MUNCH! MUNCH!

Suddenly, a little head popped out of the wooden floor between the cuckoo's feet. It was a woodworm.

"What are you doing here?" asked the cuckoo in surprise.

"I'm just having a spot of lunch," replied the worm.

"A spot of lunch?" cried the cuckoo. "Well, I certainly hope I'm not on the menu."

"A worm eating a bird? That's a funny joke," said the worm.

"Yes, hysterical," said the cuckoo. "Now, will you clear off? I have to do my next 'Cuckoo' at … at …"

The cuckoo stopped. He had lost all track of the time. Was it three o'clock yet? Usually he knew exactly what time it was, but the worm had distracted him. It was then that he heard the voices coming from the square beneath the clock.

"I missed my appointment at the hairdresser because of that cuckoo," moaned old Mrs Washenperm.

"I missed my bus!" complained Mr Snares.

"And I stayed at school an extra five minutes," groaned little Jimmy Trumpet, "and it was HORRIBLE!"

"Oh, no! Oh, no!" cried the cuckoo. "I've missed my three o'clock 'Cuckoo'!"

"It's time we got a new clock," declared Mrs Washenperm.

"Yes," agreed Mr Snares, "the cuckoo is too old."

"Why don't we get a new electric clock?" suggested little Jimmy Trumpet. "They never go wrong."

And everyone in the crowd shouted, "Yes, let's!"

So they decided to replace the cuckoo clock with an electric clock the very next day.

"I'm sorry," the cuckoo apologized to the people down in the square. "It'll never happen again."

But the people were so busy talking about the new electric clock that they didn't hear him.

Next day the workmen arrived bright and early.

"Oh, no!" cried the cuckoo. "They're going to take me away and chop me up!"

The men took out their tools and started working: HAMMER, HAMMER! SAW, SAW!

"It's all the fault of that silly worm!" cried the cuckoo.

"You called?" said the worm, popping up through one of the floorboards.

"No, I didn't call," retorted the cuckoo, "you're the very last creature I want to see right now."

"Sorry I spoke," said the worm. "I don't suppose I could nibble on a little bit more of this floor?"

The cuckoo was about to say something very rude to the worm, when he had an idea.

"If you want something to eat," he told the worm, "eat this piece of wood down here by my tail and set me free."

As the worm chomped away, little wooden balls of sweat dropped from the cuckoo. The workmen were getting nearer now. HAMMER, HAMMER! SAW, SAW!

Finally, the worm took a last bite of wood and the cuckoo was free!

"That was very tasty," said the worm, licking his tiny lips. "What's for afters?"

"You can have whatever you like," said the cuckoo. "I'm going to fly out of here."

The cuckoo started to flap his wings. They were very stiff because he had never moved them before.

HAMMER, HAMMER! SAW, SAW!

His wooden wings creaked, but the cuckoo didn't move.

HAMMER, HAMMER! SAW, SAW!

The cuckoo flapped his wings again, faster this time, but still he didn't move.

HAMMER, HAMMER! SAW, SAW!

Just as the workmen broke into the cuckoo's house, the cuckoo took off. And, as he soared into the sky, his wooden body turned into soft feathers and he became a real live bird the colour of fire.

He flew for many hours until he saw hundreds and hundreds of pointy-topped fir trees spread like a green carpet beneath him.

"That must be a forest," thought the cuckoo. "I've made it!"

And there in the forest the cuckoo lived happily ever after. He made friends with the squirrels and all the other cuckoos that lived at the tops of the green, sweet-scented trees. And if you listen carefully, you will still hear him sing, "Cuckoo! Cuckoo!" … not because he has to tell the time, but because he's free.

Inspiring Insights

- Everyone makes mistakes, even people who are usually reliable. The folk in the square should have given the cuckoo a second chance.
- Good things often come from bad situations. The worm caused a lot of trouble, but in the end he helped to set the cuckoo free.
- Sometimes we have to make a big change in our lives and this can take great courage. The cuckoo was very brave in trying out his wings and flying away.

The Kangaroo
Who Couldn't Hop

Relax, close your eyes and imagine you're in the middle of a vast, grassy plain. In the distance you can see hillsides covered with trees. It's hot and sunny and a gentle breeze is blowing. This is the story of a young kangaroo or joey, called Twitcher, who longed to do what all the other kangaroos did. But hopping didn't come easily to him. Let's listen to his story.

It was only just getting light when Twitcher inched his nose from his mother's pouch to sniff the new day. Soon all the kangaroos in his mob were up and hopping about, nibbling on leaves or scratching themselves with their front paws. Twitcher's friend Ganga climbed down from his own mother's pouch and hopped after her, searching for the sweetest new shoots.

Twitcher looked at him sadly. He couldn't hop like all the other joeys his age. He could move a bit on the ground but everyone laughed when they saw him try to move at speed.

99

When Twitcher hopped he would trip over his tail or fall flat on his tummy. Often his mother had to scoop him into her pouch and carry him like a baby. He tried to improve but it was easier to give up than be laughed at.

This morning the kangaroos were restless. It had been a long, hot summer and the bush was very dry. Everyone knew that bushfires were a risk and all the animals were afraid. Twitcher saw Thumper, the leader of their mob, turn his neck this way and then another, sniffing the air. Suddenly he called out: "Fire! Fire to the east! Get away now! Follow me to the lake at the centre of the plain!"

All the kangaroos set off immediately, bounding down the hillside. Twitcher rocked from side to side inside his mother's pouch. He could hear her panting and knew she was frightened. Now he could smell the fire, too.

Twitcher looked behind him and was terrified.

He could see orange flames dancing along the hillside, licking the trunks of trees and turning leaves into ashes. The fire was moving fast in their direction and Twitcher realized his mother wasn't keeping up with the other kangaroos.

He was slowing her down and the fire was gaining on them. There was only one thing to do.

"Mum, put me down. I've got to hop by myself," he cried and scrambled out of her pouch.

"Twitcher, climb back inside!" his mother shouted.

But he knew he could do it. He had to believe in himself.

Without a second thought Twitcher let his limbs work naturally. He found his haunches were like giant springs – once he relaxed they uncoiled and sent him flying across the plain. Soon, he and his mother reached the lake and caught their breath as they watched the fire race past them and then gradually die out. They were safe.

"You were very brave, Twitcher," said his Mum.

"I think you might become the fastest joey in the mob," said Thumper.

Twitcher just smiled.

Inspiring Insights

· Keep trying when you're learning something new, especially if you find it difficult at first. Most things come with practice.

· Remember that everyone learns things at their own pace, in their own time, when *they* are ready.

· Sometimes the hardest things become easy if you relax and stop worrying about exactly how to do them.

The Dog Who Nobody Wanted

Relax, close your eyes and imagine a street in a big city. This is a story about a dog who was lost and found on that street. He was discovered wandering all alone and was taken to a rescue centre where a lot of other stray dogs lived. He was very thin and gangly. His fur was so tangled and scruffy that the people at the rescue centre called him Rags. Let's listen to his story.

Sarah and her friend Mo worked at the dog rescue centre. It was their job to look after Rags and about 25 other dogs. They fed them twice a day, took them for walks and stroked and petted them. Although none of the dogs had a family to live with, they were all cared for very well.

Sarah had a very special relationship with Rags. Even though Rags couldn't speak, Sarah always seemed to know exactly what he was trying to say. Whenever she brought him his breakfast, he would lick the back of her hand and bark, "Thank you, Sarah! Do you want some?"

Sarah would always laugh and say, "No, thanks, Rags! I think I'll pass on the Meaty Doggy Chunks today."

"You don't know what you're missing!" Rags would bark in reply as he dived head first into his bowl.

But not everyone loved Rags the way Sarah did. People often came into the rescue centre to find a dog to take home with them. No one ever chose Rags. They thought he was too scruffy. He was the dog who nobody wanted.

"Somebody will give you a home soon, Rags," Sarah said one day, "I know they will."

Rags could only give her a sad little yelp in reply.

One morning, Sarah arrived at work to find a big fuss.

"Someone broke into the kitchen last night," said Mo, "and made a right old mess."

"Who was it?" asked Sarah.

"I've no idea," said Mo, "but they took the cans of dog food out of the cupboard and left them all over the floor."

The next night exactly the same thing happened.

"Maybe it's someone who can't afford to buy their own dog food," suggested Sarah.

"Well, I counted the cans and there aren't any missing, so whoever was trying to take them must have dropped them while trying to escape," said Mo.

"It's not right," Mo continued. "Even if the thief is poor, they shouldn't be breaking into our kitchen and stealing from us."

"I know how to find out who's doing it," said Sarah.

She borrowed a video camera from the office upstairs, and placed it out of sight in the kitchen.

"If anyone sneaks into the kitchen tonight," she thought as she pressed the record button, "they'll be caught on film."

When Sarah came into work the next day, the same thing had happened. Someone had taken the cans of dog food out of the cupboard and scattered them all over the floor.

"Let's see if the camera recorded anything," said Sarah.

She pressed the play button on the video camera and looked at the film. For a while all she could see was the empty kitchen. Then she saw the door slowly open and a shadowy shape creep into the room. It sneaked over to the cupboard and stretched up on its hind legs to reach the door knob with its front paws.

Sarah could hardly believe her eyes. It was Rags!

She watched as he opened the cupboard door and pulled out the cans. Balancing each one on his nose and gripping it between his front paws, he stacked the cans one on top of the other until he had built a tower of five.

Then he had a lot of fun knocking down the cans and chasing them as they rolled around the floor. Before he left for the night, he looked straight at the camera and gave a silly doggy grin as if he knew it was there.

"Sorry, Sarah," he seemed to be saying, "I was feeling sad and thought I'd have some midnight fun."

News soon spread of Rag's incredible doggy acrobatics and his midnight adventures were even shown on TV. Now everyone wanted to take him home. But it was Rags's turn to be choosy. He would take one look at the people who came to visit him and run off to hide in the corner.

One day, a young boy came in with his father. As soon as Rags saw him he ran to the door of his cage, opened it with his paw, and jumped into the boy's arms.

"Groover! Groover!" cried the boy.

"Do you know him?" asked Sarah.

"Yes," replied the boy. "He's my dog and his real name is Groover. I lost him last year from our circus. I thought he'd gone forever!"

"He's a circus dog?" gasped Sarah.

"Yes," replied the boy. "And he's the best! Aren't you, Groover?"

"Yes!" barked Groover, and he got up on his hind legs and started doing a little doggy dance.

"He's amazing!" laughed Mo.

"Thank you for looking after him so well," said the boy's father. "I don't know how we can repay you."

"I think I do," said the boy with a smile, and Groover gave a happy little bark.

That Saturday, Sarah and Mo were sitting in the best seats in a big circus tent. They were watching the star of the show: Groover the Wonder Dog.

"Woof! Woof!" barked Groover as he jumped and caught a ball on his nose. Everyone in the audience clapped and cheered. Groover had found his home at last. Now he was the dog who everybody wanted.

Inspiring Insights

- Animals need to be loved like you and me. Always look after them, just like Sarah cared for Groover.
- Appearances are not always important. Try not to judge people or animals just by the way they look.
- Even if a situation seems hopeless now, life is full of changes. Be patient and you'll find that things get better.

The Phoenix and the Blacksmith's Boy

Relax, be very still and imagine a fiery phoenix – a very beautiful bird with gold, red and orange plumage that is said to live for hundreds of years. The phoenix in this story built her nest a long, long time ago in the brickwork of a blacksmith's forge. Let's listen to her story.

"What a beautiful bird!" said the blacksmith, who never ceased admiring her. "Her feathers are like flames."

The phoenix was impressed with the blacksmith, too, and enjoyed watching him work.

He plunged a rod of metal into the blazing fire at the centre of the forge. When it glowed red as sunset he pulled it from the flames and beat it flat until he had made a gleaming sword.

"A fine craftsman," thought the phoenix. "Any knight would be proud to fight with that sword."

"I must deliver this," called the blacksmith to a small boy in ragged clothes.

"Watch the fire, Tom. And try to make a spade while I'm out delivering this sword."

Tom staggered forward with a rod of iron but was barely able to lift it high enough to reach the flames.

"Ha!" squawked the phoenix. The scruffy boy was useless!

Tom leapt backward, dropping the iron bar on his toe.

"You'll never make a sword for a knight if you can't even make a spade!" jeered the phoenix.

Hopping on one foot, Tom plunged the bar into the flames.

"I'll show you!" he said. He beat the glowing metal flat with a hammer, making the leaf-like shape of a spade.

But Tom's arms ached and smoke stung his eyes. Suddenly, there was a great CLANG!

By mistake, Tom had hit the edge of the metal with the heavy hammer and twisted it. No one could dig with a spade like that. Sparks flew as Tom tried to beat it back into shape.

"Hopeless!" laughed the phoenix but then all of a sudden her nest burst into flames. The bird and her nest were reduced to a pile of silver ash.

"Oh no!" gasped Tom. Had his sparks caused the fire?

When the blacksmith returned, he looked at Tom's work.

"Try again," he said gently. "You'll get the hang of it."

Tom didn't mention how the bird had teased him

or how he thought he'd set her alight. All winter he worked hard. Soon he was able to make a spade and a pitchfork, too. Then in spring, while the blacksmith was at market, Tom made a sword. He beat the metal, pointing it like the sharp beak of the phoenix.

"Splendid!" said a voice above him. The phoenix peered at the magnificent sword. "I'm glad I could return and see your work again. I'm sorry I was cruel. I judged you too soon."

"You're alive …" gasped Tom.

"I'm a phoenix," chuckled the bird. "We're reborn from the ashes time after time."

"Like making something new in a fire?" asked Tom.

"Just as a fine blacksmith does," said the phoenix. "Just like you, Tom."

Inspiring Insights

- If you do or say something wrong, it's important to find a way to apologize. The phoenix is glad she has a second chance to put things right with Tom.
- New skills are difficult when we first learn them. Be patient! Don't expect to be good at something straightaway.
- Kind words from others help us to believe in ourselves. With encouragement from the blacksmith, Tom keeps trying until he can make difficult things.

The Lucky
Narwhal

Relax, be very still and imagine an extraordinary creature called a narwhal. Narwhals are a special type of whale and each one has a long horn on its head like a unicorn. This is a story about a young narwhal called Spike and his friend Marina the mermaid. Let's listen to their story.

"Oh Spike!" said Marina, swimming alongside the friendly narwhal one day. "King Neptune is having a concert. I've been asked to sing a solo."

"That's wonderful!" said Spike. "You love singing."

"I do," agreed Marina, "but I get so nervous. I just know I'll make a mess of it."

"No you won't!" laughed Spike, splashing Marina with his tail. "You've such a beautiful voice and you practise hard every day."

"Come to the concert with me," pleaded Marina.

"You could be my lucky mascot," she said, grabbing hold of Spike's tail and letting him pull her along.

"Good things always happen when you're around, Spike. Remember the time when we found the pearl bracelet my mother had lost?" Marina continued.

"Only because we were playing hide-and-seek and you were hiding behind the rock where she'd dropped it," giggled Spike.

"Or the time we saved Old Jock, the fisherman, from drowning?" said Marina.

"Old Jock was only drowning because you tickled me so hard I splashed my tail and tipped him out of his little green boat!" Spike reminded her.

They both laughed as they remembered the fisherman's surprised face.

"You see, Spike, you bring everyone luck!" declared Marina. "You're like a magical unicorn of the sea!"

"A MAGICAL UNICORN OF THE SEA!" Spike repeated, rolling onto his back. "I like the sound of that."

"So will you come to the concert?" asked Marina. "I know you'll bring me good luck."

"I promise," said Spike. "But now I'd better hurry home for tea. If I'm lucky it'll be my favourite ... squid soup!"

But, on the evening of the concert, something dreadful happened. Spike had swum far across the ocean to play.

When he poked his head above the waves, he saw the sun sinking low in the sky.

"Time to head back!" he said. "I can't be late for Marina's concert. I'm her lucky mascot!" Splashing his tail, he sped off. But he was so busy hurrying to King Neptune's cave that he wasn't looking where he was going.

"Ah!" cried Spike as he felt a sharp tug on his tail. He had swum right into a fisherman's net. He tried to swim away but the harder he tugged, the tighter the net pulled around him. His splendid horn was all caught up, like a knitting needle in a ball of tangled wool.

"I'll never make it to Marina's concert now!" Spike groaned. "She'll be so nervous if she sees I'm not there to bring her luck."

Spike tugged harder still. The net grew tighter.

"I'm the unluckiest narwhal in the world," he sobbed. "Now I'll never hear Marina sing. I'll never escape from this net! Never!"

But, just at that moment, Spike saw the bottom of a little green boat floating above his head.

I know that boat, he thought excitedly. That must be Old Jock, the sailor. The one Marina and I rescued when he fell into the sea.

"Help me!" cried Spike. "Please!" He wriggled as hard as he could so that his long horn tapped the bottom of the boat.

"Spike," cried Jock, grabbing his sharp fisherman's knife and trying to cut the little narwhal free. "You're in a tangle."

"Hurry, please," cried Spike. "I'm going to be a lucky mascot at Marina's concert."

"You? Lucky?" laughed the old fisherman. "You don't look lucky to me. Not when you're all tangled up in this net!"

"Well, I am certainly lucky you came along and saved me," said Spike, as the net was cut free. "Thank you, Jock." He leapt high above the waves and arched his tail.

It was sunset. There wasn't a moment to lose. King Neptune's concert would be starting any minute.

Just as the first notes of music bubbled through the water, Spike swam into King Neptune's cave.

As she was opening her mouth to sing, Marina spotted him and smiled.

As her voice rose up, Spike realized something. He was glad he had come to the concert because he loved to hear Marina sing. But she didn't need him for good luck. Not really. She would be brilliant anyway.

Sure enough, her song was the highlight of the evening.

She sang out loud and clear and calm.

"Beautiful!" cried King Neptune when she was done. Crabs and lobsters clapped their claws as the crowd cheered and splashed. Spike splashed loudest of all.

"Bravo!" he whooped.

When the concert was over, Spike told Marina all about his lucky escape from the net and how Jock had rescued him.

"Goodness!" gasped Marina. "I'm surprised you had any luck left over for me."

"You didn't need it," smiled Spike. "You have a beautiful voice and you work really hard. That's what made the difference … not having me here as a lucky mascot."

"Thank you," said Marina, flinging her arms round him. "I know one thing … I'm lucky to have a friend like you!"

Inspiring Insights

- Luck doesn't really help us to face a challenge – hard work and practice is the best preparation.
- Sometimes it's not possible for people you love to come to an important event. Don't be cross or sad if this happens. Knowing that they love you and are thinking of you will give you confidence to do your best.
- Even if you are in a hurry, take care and pay attention to your surroundings.

The Silver Hare

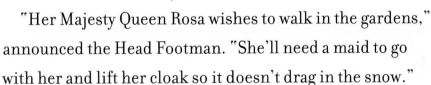

R elax, be very still and imagine a palace surrounded by beautiful gardens. This is a story about a servant girl called Holly, a queen and a silver hare. A hare looks like a big rabbit, only its ears are longer than a rabbit's and it has stronger legs and larger feet to help it run really fast. Let's listen to their story.

"Her Majesty Queen Rosa wishes to walk in the gardens," announced the Head Footman. "She'll need a maid to go with her and lift her cloak so it doesn't drag in the snow."

"I'll help," blushed Holly. She'd only been working in the palace for a week and the Head Footman, with his gruff voice and long, curly moustache, frightened her.

"I love gardens," she explained.

"Queen Rosa is waiting in the hall," said the Footman. "But remember, don't speak until she speaks to you."

"And don't let her cloak drag on the ground, young lady," warned Cook.

"And don't ever mention poor King Alban!" said the Footman seriously.

"Gracious no!" gasped Cook. "Ever since King Alban died ten years ago, no-one has talked of him. Queen Rosa loved her husband dearly and must not be reminded of her sadness now."

Holly thought it strange not to speak about someone you love, but before she could ask any questions the Footman clapped his hands.

"Hurry along! Don't keep Her Majesty waiting."

The old queen walked quietly through the gardens. Holly followed three steps behind, taking care not to let Queen Rosa's blue velvet cloak drag on the ground.

"Such a beautiful afternoon," smiled Queen Rosa.

Holly nodded but she didn't answer. She wasn't sure if it would be right to speak. Was Queen Rosa talking to her? Or was she just thinking aloud?

It felt strange not to talk, though. Holly would have liked to point to the icy lily pond and say how pretty it was.

"How these have grown." said Queen Rosa. She stopped in a circle of trees around a fountain. "They're …"

"Holly trees … " interrupted Holly before she could stop herself. She hadn't meant to speak.

"I'm sorry," her hands flew to her mouth. "It's just, that's my name you see … Holly."

"A very pretty name it is, too," smiled Queen Rosa.

"Oh dear!" Holly looked at her feet. In her embarrassment she'd dropped the edge of the cloak. It was dragging along the ground.

"Don't worry," urged Queen Rosa. "Come, take my arm."

Holly smiled. Queen Rosa was so kind and friendly – not stern like she'd expected.

"My husband planted these trees," Queen Rosa explained.

"King Alban?" said Holly. Then she gasped again. How stupid! How could she have mentioned his name?

But Queen Rosa nodded. "They were a gift the first Christmas we were married."

"How lovely!" said Holly.

"You'll never guess what he used to do," chuckled Queen Rosa. "His favourite trick was to put a sprig of holly on my chair before I sat down for Christmas dinner."

"Ouch!" Holly giggled. "The prickles must have hurt a bit."

"They did!" Queen Rosa's face was alight with laughter now and though her skin was wrinkled and her hair was grey, her blue eyes sparkled like sapphires.

"He loved playing tricks," said Queen Rosa. "Silly thing!"

Holly smiled. She knew Queen Rosa was joking ... in fact, talking about King Alban didn't seem to make her sad at all.

"He was a great leader too, of course," said Queen Rosa. "He stopped the wars in the northern lands and gave the poor farmers money for seeds. But do you know what I remember him for?"

Holly shook her head.

"I remember how he used to put his bedroom slippers on the wrong feet!" Queen Rosa roared with laughter. "He'd stand there, rubbing his eyes. Then he'd lift each foot and stare at it, as if he couldn't quite work out what was wrong!"

Queen Rosa and Holly reached the bottom of the path. As they turned back toward the holly trees they were quiet for a moment. Suddenly, Holly squeezed Queen Rosa's arm.

"Look, Your Majesty," she whispered.

Standing beside the fountain was a silver hare with long, silky ears and twitching whiskers.

"Isn't he magnificent?" whispered Queen Rosa.

The hare stood on his hind legs and stared at them. Then he did the strangest thing. He rubbed his eyes and lifted each foot to look at it, as if something wasn't quite right ...

"It's as if he's put his slippers on wrong!" gasped Holly.

Tears rolled down Queen Rosa's cheeks.

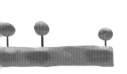

"Take care," she called as the hare bounded away.

"I'm sorry, Your Majesty. You're sad now," said Holly. "It's all my fault. I shouldn't have spoken about King Alban."

"No. I'm crying because I'm happy," said Queen Rosa. "I have fond memories. No one ever mentions Alban and I wish they would. I miss him so much. But I don't want to forget him. I want to remember him just as he was."

"You can talk to me about King Alban whenever you like," said Holly, boldly.

"Good!" said Queen Rosa, wiping her eyes. "Let's meet here again tomorrow, then. I'd like to look for that hare. He was so like Alban, it was almost as if it was a sign."

"To show he remembers you, too?" asked Holly.

"Exactly!" smiled Queen Rosa.

Inspiring Insights

⬦⬦⬦⬦⬦⬦⬦⬦⬦⬦⬦⬦⬦⬦⬦

- It's always sad when a loved one dies – but it doesn't mean we should never talk about that person. Happy memories are a wonderful thing.
- Grown-ups sometimes need to cry or to laugh, just like children do. Having feelings is part of being able to love others.
- If you feel sad, it helps to talk to someone. Always let a person you trust know if you have a problem or feel unhappy.

Tortoise's Birthday Trip

Relax, be very still and imagine a small garden with a great apple tree. At the far end of the garden lies a large green field that leads to the hills. This is a story about two tortoises that live in that garden and their friend Daisy, a cheerful brown horse. Let's listen to their story.

The tortoises living in the garden were gentle creatures that couldn't go very far or move very quickly. Cecil was 50 years old, which is very young by tortoise standards. He had a crinkly little head that poked out of his large shell. The other tortoise was so old that he had forgotten his name. So he called himself Tortoise, because he knew that this was a name he would never forget. Tortoise had even forgotten how old he was.

Every year on his birthday, Cecil would ask him, "How old are you, Tortoise?"

And Tortoise would reply with a smile, "A year older than the last time you asked."

125

Cecil loved looking after Tortoise. He collected soft leaves for his bed. He made sure that the branches above his head covered him when it rained. And he always rolled a juicy apple up the garden for Tortoise's breakfast.

Every day, Cecil would watch Tortoise move slowly to a little hole in the fence. Sometimes he would talk to Daisy, as she chewed grass in the field. Sometimes he would sit in silence for hours, peering through his spectacles.

"Why do you sit here all the time?" asked Cecil.

"I like looking at that hill over there," replied Tortoise.

"But why?" asked Cecil. "It's only a hill, isn't it?"

"It may be just a hill, but I like imagining what lies beyond it," replied Tortoise. "I've lived in this garden all my life and I've been very happy here, but sometimes I wonder what it would be like to go out and explore the world. Just for one day."

Cecil thought about what Tortoise had said. It would be exciting to go and see the world beyond the garden, but how could they ever manage it?

"We'll need help," thought Cecil. "I know just who to ask."

On the morning of Tortoise's birthday Cecil woke up extra early. He found the biggest, reddest apple beneath the apple tree and rolled it slowly up the garden.

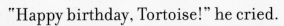

"Happy birthday, Tortoise!" he cried.

"Thank you," said Tortoise. "Is that enormous red apple for me?"

"Well," said Cecil. "It is and it isn't. You're going to have to share it with somebody today."

A loud neigh came from the other side of the fence.

"Yes," said Daisy, "with me!"

"I didn't know it was your birthday, too," said Tortoise.

"It isn't," explained Daisy, "but if you two want me to take you to the top of the hill, I'm going to need something more for my breakfast than the hay the farmer gives me."

"We're going to the top of the hill?" enquired Tortoise, sounding astonished. "But how will you get us there?"

"I'll carry you on my back, of course," replied Daisy. "Now eat up your half of the apple!"

Tortoise hardly ate any of the apple because he was too excited. When Daisy had finished munching, she lowered her head to the hole in the fence.

"Climb onto my nose," she instructed Tortoise and Cecil, "and I'll place you on my back."

When the two tortoises were sitting comfortably, Daisy whinnied, "Hold on tight!" And she started trotting gently up the hill.

"I haven't had so much fun for about a hundred years!" laughed Tortoise.

"It'll be even better when we get to the top!" smiled Daisy.

"Are we nearly there?" asked Cecil.

"Not far now," replied Daisy. "We just have to go through that gate ahead."

Cecil could see a wooden fence with a gate near the top of the hill.

"Oh, no!" cried Daisy. "The gate is closed."

"Does that mean we can't go to the top of the hill?" asked Tortoise in a disappointed voice.

"Not if I can help it," said Daisy. "Hold on tight!"

Daisy gave a determined swish of her tail and started to go faster and faster until she was speeding along at a full gallop … and then she jumped! For one wonderful moment Cecil and Tortoise felt as if they were hanging in the air. Then, bump! Daisy landed on the other side of the fence with the two friends still clinging onto her back.

"We were flying!" cried Cecil.

"Like birds!" shouted Tortoise. "We're nearly there!"

The words had hardly left his mouth when the smell of crisp salt air wafted over the top of the hill and they saw the most amazing sight ever!

"Oh, my goodness!" exclaimed Tortoise. "I've never seen so much water in my life!"

"It's the sea," said Daisy.

They stood in silence and watched the waves crashing upon the shore as the water sparkled in the sunlight.

"Oh! Thank you! This is wonderful!" Tortoise almost jumped for joy. "I feel a hundred years younger!"

"And that would make you how old?" asked Cecil.

"A year older than the last time you asked," chuckled Tortoise in reply.

"Happy birthday to you!" sang Cecil and Daisy.

"It's the best birthday I've ever had!" beamed Tortoise. And it was. It was the day that Tortoise left the garden and saw the world.

Inspiring Insights

- Taking care of those who are older – and perhaps more fragile – than us is a good and kind thing to do. Cecil takes very good care of his older friend Tortoise by bringing him an apple for breakfast every morning.
- The best presents are often ones that come from the heart. Thoughtfulness and care in choosing or making a gift make it extra special.
- Saying "thank you" is one of the best ways to show how grateful you are.

The Noisy Bird

Relax, close your eyes and imagine a town in a distant time and place. Bandits roam the streets, stealing things from people's houses and robbing anyone unlucky enough to come across them. This is a story about a clever bird that saved a sleepy town. Let's listen to his story.

Long ago, many towns had strong walls to protect the inhabitants from enemies and it was the job of the night watchman to guard the gateway after dark.

The trouble with the watchman in this story – whose name was Mr Peerless – was that he liked to have a nice meat pie for his supper and a snooze at 11 o'clock.

"Nothing ever happens, anyway," he reassured Mrs Peerless, his wife. "It's the middle of the night. Everybody knows that the gate to the town is locked."

"But what if bandits creep over the walls to steal our riches?" asked Mrs Peerless, clutching a silver brooch her mother had given to her.

"Bandits won't come!" scoffed Mr Peerless.

Night after night he dozed undisturbed. Then one spring evening a scruffy looking bird with long, brown feathers came to roost on the town gatepost.

"What a plain looking thing you are!" laughed Mr Peerless and he closed his eyes.

In the middle of the night, the bird began to squawk.

"Hush!" groaned Mr Peerless, opening one eye. "Be quiet or I'll bake you in a pie!"

But the bird squawked again.

Mr Peerless threw a stone. "Go to sleep, silly bird!"

But the bird flapped and squawked even louder.

"Ark!" it cried in its shrill voice. "ARK! ARK!"

"Tomorrow morning, I'll buy a bow and arrow and shoot you," hissed Mr Peerless, sleepily. He closed his eyes and pulled his hat down low on his head.

But the bird kept squawking and it wasn't long before the whole town was awake.

The Mayor looked out of his bedroom window.

A gang of bandits was climbing over the town gate.

"Guards, seize them!" shouted the Mayor.

Even Mr Peerless heard the commotion now.

"I must have dozed off!" he gasped.

"You didn't even see us coming!" sneered the bandits, as they were led away to prison. "If it wasn't for that noisy bird, we'd have crept into town and stolen all your jewels."

In the morning, the Mayor announced that the bird should have a reward. He opened the town treasure chest and scooped out a handful of precious gems.

But jewels were of no use to the bird. He scratched at them in the dust and tried to eat them … but then a very strange thing happened. His long tail feathers began shimmering with turquoise and ruby and gold.

Mr Peerless dropped his pie. "You're beautiful!" he cried.

"Ark!" The bird spread his feathers proudly like a fan.

… And perhaps that is how the peacock got his magnificent tail.

Inspiring Insights

◇◇◇◇◇◇◇◇◇◇◇◇◇◇◇◇◇

- If you take pride in your work, you'll enjoy it more – the plain bird did a good deed and got bright feathers as his reward.
- Always try your best to take your responsibilities seriously – Mr Peerless can't be bothered to do a good job and lets everyone down.
- If you have something important to say, don't let others put you off – just like the bird didn't let Mr Peerless bully him and kept squawking his warning.

Taking the Stories Further

Visualization is conjuring up pictures in your mind at will. Meditation means learning to still your mind so that you become calm and gain greater focus. Learning to visualize and meditate will help your child gain self-confidence and empathy, as well as improving his concentration and creativity. The visualization and meditations that follow use the stories within this collection as a starting point for your child to immerse himself in the natural world and take himself off on imaginative adventures with delightful animal guides.

Over time, these visualizations will help your child to use the same techniques to face any challenging situation that calls for courage and serenity. For example, visualizing himself doing well in an exam or playing brilliantly at a music recital will improve his performance. Many top athletes also use visualization in this way to improve their performances and your child will enjoy hearing success stories based on a practice he can do daily. Like all skills, visualization is easier and more effective the more we practise it. Many children enjoy visualization games. Try showing your child an unusual object and then asking him to close his eyes and describe it in as much detail as possible. Or you could ask him to describe an imaginary journey taken along a river down to the sea.

Remember that visualization doesn't just have to be about seeing: you can ask your child to imagine smells, sounds, feelings and tastes, too. This will all help bring the stories alive for him. However, the illustrations that accompany each story are a good place to start.

Encouraging your child's ability to use imaginative thinking is a gift that he will cherish throughout his life. It is also good to note that daydreaming is not wasting time but is, in fact, a vital tool at our disposal for gaining greater insight into our hopes and dreams. Psychologists have also found that habitual daydreamers have better working memories, so there is a good cognitive reason for giving your child's imagination free rein.

Make it a bedtime ritual to do a relaxing visualization or meditation and you'll soon both benefit from the calming effect of a little journey into the more creative regions of the mind each night.

Meeting an Animal Guide

Sit with your child cross-legged on the floor, bodies relaxed, and spend a few minutes breathing deeply together. Ask your child to close her eyes and then read the following guided visualization to her.

"Imagine yourself sitting on a rock shelf high above a steep-sided valley. A river winds its way along the valley floor, and pine trees cloak the sides of the valley. Up on the rock shelf you are safe and secure and you have a bird's eye view of everything below you. The wind whistles around you and in the distance you can hear the sound of the river rushing over boulders as its drops down the valley.

"You are sitting within a circle of stones and are facing the rising sun. In front of you lies a white feather. At the right of you lies a seashell. Behind you lies the skin of a snake and to the left of you is some animal fur. You are on a vision quest – a sacred journey to uncover the animal that is your spirit guide. This animal is your special friend; a wise companion who is being sent to you to ensure your safe path through life. Only you will see your guide because it is for your eyes alone. Continue to breathe deeply and regularly. Listen to the whistling of the wind around you and the

sound of the rushing river. You are safe on your rock shelf
and are now standing inside the stone circle. Begin to spin
slowly inside your circle. You are perfectly safe and well.
Close your eyes and begin to spin a little faster now. As you
spin, the feather, the seashell, the snakeskin and the fur all
appear before you, one by one.

"Stop spinning now. You are no longer alone inside your
stone circle. An animal stands before you, but only you can
see it. It could be a bird, a mammal, a reptile, an insect or it
could even be a fish – because this is your spirit guide and
anything is possible. You can see your animal guide clearly.
It nods its head towards you gently and then it gives you a
special message, for you alone.

"Once you've received your message, thank your animal
guide for appearing before you. Your guide now departs and
you wave goodbye to him or her. Then wiggle your toes and
fingers; know that you are safe and back sitting at home.
Slowly open your eyes and return to the room."

Earth Meditation

Sit quietly with your child in a comfortable position. Take three deep breaths together, ensuring that you are both calm and relaxed. Asking your child to keep his eyes closed, read the following meditation to him.

"Imagine you are standing in a deep forest. Tall trees stretch up above you and ferns and bracken line the path on which you're standing. A twig snaps behind you and you turn to catch a glimpse of an animal disappearing along the trail. You can't quite make out the animal so you must carefully follow it, being sure not to frighten or disturb it. The quieter and more respectful you are, the more you'll see and the more you will learn.

"Make your way down the path carefully and, gradually, the shape of the animal becomes clearer to you. You can make out its hind legs now and you can see what kind of animal it is. The animal has a gift for you, but it will only be given if you are gentle and kind – for the animal scares easily and distrusts humans. You must be as quiet as a mouse in order to win the trust of this rare and beautiful animal. The animal leads you further into the forest and you start to see more and more of the animal.

"You can see all of its body now and the back of its head. But still the animal is fearful and is not ready to give its gift yet. You must show that you are patient and willing to be led by the animal at its own pace.

Finally the animal leads you to a clearing. Sunlight falls in shafts through the trees and birds are softly chirping in the branches. There is a small, still pond in the centre of the clearing. The animal hesitates then makes its way towards the pond. It bends down to drink. It turns its head towards you and beckons you to drink too. You slowly approach and drink beside your shy friend.

"And this is the great gift you've been given. Because you've been so gentle and kind and respectful, a beautiful wild animal has allowed you to share its world. Not everyone is allowed to get so close and to make friends with these wonderful animals.

"You can now slowly walk back along the forest path to where your journey began. Take a few deep breaths and slowly open your eyes."

Air Meditation

Sit quietly with your child, breathing deeply. Ask her to close her eyes and relax and read the following meditation out loud to her.

"Imagine you're sitting high up in the branches of a very tall tree. You're perfectly safe and have nothing to fear at all. A gentle wind is blowing and the branch sways beneath you, but you're not afraid. You're enjoying the wind lifting your hair and the blue sky stretching out above you.

"Suddenly you hear a whooshing sound and an enormous bird alights on the branch beside you. The bird turns toward you and it's clear it wants you to climb on its back. Without any hesitation, you wrap your legs around the fluffy feathered tummy and hold on tight.

"You take off and it's thrilling! You sail through the air, swooping through branches and skimming the tops of leaves. You circle up towards the clouds, and then dive down again to the forest. The whole time you are laughing with joy because it's so exciting and wonderful.

"At last the bird returns to the branch and you safely climbs off. Thank the bird for such a wonderful ride. Slowly Take some deep breaths and open your eyes."

Sea Meditation

Sit quietly with your child, breathing deeply together. Ask your child to close his eyes and relax. Then read the following meditation out loud to him.

"Imagine you're by the seashore looking out to the horizon. Waves are lapping at your feet and the water is deliciously warm. You enter the water and are able to swim strongly. You duck-dive under the waves, coming face-to-face with a turtle. The turtle beckons you on and you follow, until you reach the edge of a beautiful coral reef. You can see the pinks, reds and purples of the coral fluttering like grasses in the current. You see brightly striped fish – gold and blue and green – darting amongst the coral. It is a beautiful world but the turtle leads you on – you are now swimming out to a great ocean and passing sharks, dugongs, octopus and stingrays. You stay close to the turtle who protects you and tells you there is nothing to fear.

"Suddenly you encounter a great whale that has silently appeared behind you. It is the size of a house and it is magnificent. You and the turtle swim respectfully at a distance admiring its power and grace. It is time to return home now. Take some deep breaths. Slowly open your eyes."

Index of Values and Issues

These two complementary indexes cover the specific topics that the 20 stories in this book are designed to address directly or by implication. The same topics are covered from two different perspectives: positive (Values) and negative (Issues). Each index reference consists of an abbreviated story title, followed by the page number on which the story begins.

Acknowledgments

The Publishers would like to thank the three storytellers for writing the tales listed below:

Lou Kuenzler
"The Acacia Tree Friends", "Jojo's Journey", "The Lucky Narwhal", "The Night Flight",
"The Noisy Bird ", "The Silver Hare", "The Smallest Pony", "The Phoenix and
the Blacksmith's Boy"

Sandra Rigby
"The Extra-Slow Wombat", "The Flight of the Condor", "Gopal and the Mermaid",
"The Kangaroo Who Couldn't Hop", "The Lonely Dragon", "The Princess and the Unicorn"

Andrew Weale
"The Brave Little Firefly", "Cedric the Centipede", "The Cuckoo and the Worm",
"The Dog Who Nobody Wanted", "Little Black Bear and the Big Sleep",
"Tortoise's Birthday Trip"